CW01648462

# THE GIRL WITH AMBER EYES

Sue Johnson

TOADSTONE PRESS

The Girl With Amber Eyes



This edition 2019
published by Toadstone Press
ISBN: 9781912869015



Previously published as a
My Weekly Pocket Novel

# THE GIRL WITH AMBER EYES

Sue Johnson

PROLOGUE

14th February 1946

It was a pink and gold morning full of promise. Ada Wilson stood shivering more with excitement than cold on the London platform of the little station in Marchwood.

Her luggage was at her feet, she was wearing her black velvet Sunday hat with the pink roses on it and her best coat and gloves.

Any minute now Jack would be with her. She'd feel his warm breath on her cheek ruffling her dark hair, his hand in hers. Ada felt a thrill of anticipation.

The seven o'clock train came and went in a flurry of jarring metal and steam. As the coal scent of the engine died away, Ada began to feel uneasy.

"Be early," Jack had said. "We'll get away before anybody misses us and starts creating a fuss. Don't forget to bring the necklace I gave you."

As if she would! He'd given her the filigree silver and ruby necklace on her birthday the previous week. They'd met in the little circular folly between the woods and the church. It was late afternoon and so cold their breath showed in white clouds. Her fingers felt numb as she untied the ribbon on the rectangular package he'd given her. She folded back the paper and stared at the wooden box, noticed the smell of sandalwood.

"Aren't you going to open it?" he'd teased, his eyes soft with love.

Ada lifted the lid and gasped. Cradled by the black velvet lining was a necklace finer than anything she'd ever seen. It was filigree silver with rubies the size of pear drops. Ruby was her middle name.

"Look on it as an engagement ring for now," he'd said.

They'd sat in the folly sharing kisses and the rock cakes she'd made, looking through the trees towards Oakwood House where, on this late winter's afternoon, the downstairs windows showed soft golden light.

"It is alright for me to have this, isn't it?" she'd asked, indicating the box on her lap that she couldn't believe was hers.

"Of course it is," he said. "I am Jack Kingsley, youngest son of Edward and Mary Kingsley of Oakwood House. Wherever we are in the world I will still be Jack Kingsley and you will be my wife."

He'd silenced her with a soft kiss.

Ada knew he didn't get on well with his father and older brothers. He greatly resented being the youngest son and the fact that Oakwood House would never belong to him. That was why he'd persuaded her to elope with him.

"You are sure?" he'd asked her yesterday. "You will be there at the station waiting for me?"

Ada looked around uneasily wondering what had gone wrong. She had a terrible feeling that he was the one who'd changed his mind.

Ada had waited until her mother had gone out to her early morning cleaning job. Her father had died in the war and she felt bad that her mother would suffer hardship without the money she gave her from her job in the local cinema. As soon as she and Jack were settled wherever they were going, she'd send her mother some money and maybe an invitation to join them.

Frank Brookes, the porter, eyed her curiously and then went back to sweeping the platform one slow inch at a time. Ada had known him since they'd been at school together. She asked him if anyone had been here waiting before she arrived.

He shook his head. "No one before you Ada," he said.

By the time she finally gave up all hope of Jack showing up, her whole body ached with cold. The golden light had faded and the sky was now a sickly shade of yellow that promised snow. She walked slowly home with her luggage. Luckily her mother was still out working so she didn't have to explain anything.

Feeling hurt and bewildered, she pushed her case to the back of the cupboard in her bedroom. She lifted the loose floorboard under her bed and hid the box with the necklace in it.

She went downstairs and made a pot of tea, sat nursing the cup between her cold fingers. Her heart felt numb. She loved Jack so much and he'd betrayed her.

It wasn't until the following day the news filtered through that Jack Kingsley, aged 35, of Oakwood House had been found dead of a heart attack in his bedroom early on the morning of $14^{th}$ February.

Ada, who could barely wait a few hours to see him again would never see his smile light up his blue eyes or feel the touch of his hand on hers.

# CHAPTER ONE

June 2016

As the train carried her north, Emily Randall felt her heart sink a little further with each mile. Everyone else on the train seemed busy and upbeat. There were several young couples sharing secret smiles and families with sleepy children returning from a day out. Even the chatty silver haired lady sitting next to her was looking forward to being met by somebody when she reached the end of her journey.

Emily had no such expectation. Her luggage was on the rack above her – a battered blue suitcase and a series of carrier bags with clothing spilling from them. She'd sold most of her art stuff to buy her train ticket. From having a clear idea of where her life was going, she now had no idea what would happen next.

Within a few days, Emily's dreams had unravelled like a badly knitted jumper. Only one thing was certain, she needed to get away from London.

She'd contacted her mother who'd made it clear she couldn't help her. She was now living in Spain with her new husband.

"None of this would have happened if you'd done the Business Studies course like I wanted you to," she said. "Didn't I warn you that artistic types were untrustworthy?"

Emily could imagine her mother Kate's immaculately made up face and scarlet lipstick and her ultra-tidy house with not so much as a cushion out of place. Artwork was chosen by an interior designer because it matched the colour of the walls, not because the pictures inspired Kate in any way.

The only place Emily felt certain of a welcome was with her grandmother. She felt bad that she hadn't been able to let her know she was coming, but ninety-year-old Ada steadfastly refused to have a phone and Emily had been in too much of a state before she left London to look for the lady next door's number.

The view from the window changed from grey, dusty city buildings to fields edged with wild roses and elderflower. The train sped past cottages like the one she imagined living in with James. She saw children playing in fields and fishing in shallow streams and thought sadly of all her faded dreams. On a few occasions her fingers reached automatically for the sketchbook and pencil she always carried in her red velvet shoulder-bag before she quickly repressed the urge. To draw anything at the moment would only remind her of all she'd lost.

She huddled in her seat in the corner of the carriage by the window. She was wearing sunglasses to disguise eyes that were red from crying and dark circled from lack of sleep. The coffee she'd bought at Paddington was the only thing she'd had all day and her stomach growled with emptiness. Emily knew she didn't function well without food, but found herself incapable of eating when she was upset.

With a mixture of anxiety and relief, she heard the announcement over the tannoy that the next station was Marchwood. *'Marchwood has a short platform. Would any passengers alighting please leave from carriages A, B or C.'*

The train slowed down. Emily stood up and collected her belongings from the overhead rack, trying not to spill any contents from the bags. A young man stood up to help her. She thanked him with a polite smile, noticed the flare of interest in his dark eyes as they flicked over her slim body in red t-shirt and jeans. At one time, she'd have returned his flirtatious look. Now she just wanted to get off the train. It would be a long time, if ever, before she trusted a man again.

The station looked the same as she remembered it with its hanging baskets of scarlet geraniums and indigo lobelia and carefully tended rose garden. She and Gran hadn't used the station on their trips out together because Gran said she didn't like travelling by train. After Granddad Frank died and his old Morris Minor was sold, they used to go on the bus to Worcester or Malvern.

It felt uncomfortably hot out on the platform after the air conditioned train. Emily's hastily packed bags were beginning to split and she hoped she'd get them the short distance to Gran's house before they completely fell apart. She put them down on a bench to try and sort things out. The scent of roses and lavender drifted towards her on the warm breeze.

*James had bought her roses the first time they went out to dinner…*

No, she wouldn't allow herself to think about how things used to be.

Emily took her sunglasses off to mop her brimming eyes. The sun's glare startled her – as did the fact that life was going on around her. She put the sunglasses back on, picked up her bags and headed towards the exit. As she did so, she collided with a harassed looking woman in a floppy pink hat coming the other way. Emily dropped the bag with her undies in it to the amusement of a group of teenage boys who had also just arrived on the platform.

"I'm so sorry," said the woman, doing her best to cram Emily's things back into the bag. "It must be the heat. I'm not usually so clumsy."

"It doesn't matter," said Emily.

The woman had pushed her hat back, showing short blonde hair.

"I thought I recognised you," she said. "Emily, what are you doing here? Auntie Molly said you were blazing a trail down in London. Why haven't they put out the red carpet for you?"

"Angie!" said Emily, not feeling as if she had the energy to explain anything at the moment.

Angie rattled on, not expecting her to answer. Emily was glad when an announcement over the loudspeaker said the next train was just arriving and she could make her escape.

"We must catch up if you're here for a few days," said Angie, blowing her a kiss. "I want to hear everything about your latest successes." She put a glossy leaflet on the top of one of Emily's bags. "I'm dying to catch up over tea and cakes and tell you about my new café – mind you, me and close proximity to food does nothing for the waist line. You're lucky you've always managed to stay slim." She hurried in the direction of the train and Emily was left with the usual feeling she got when she was with Angie – of being buffeted by a whirlwind.

She felt a stab of envy that Angie seemed to be succeeding with her dreams whereas her life had gone so horribly wrong.

Emily was thankful not to meet anyone else on the short walk to Gran's house. Laurel Terrace looked older and shabbier than it had before. Several houses were empty with overgrown front gardens and peeling paintwork. Gran's still looked clean and neat, the net curtains sparkling white.

The front gate creaked as Emily pushed it open. She walked the few strides to the front door between towering pink and yellow hollyhocks, then knocked on the front door and heard Ada's muffled footsteps on the wooden floor of the hall.

"If you're trying to sell anything then go away," came Ada's clear voice from the other side of the door. "And watch out for the cat, he's a demon."

Emily smiled for the first time in several days. Nelson, Ada's one-eyed ginger tom was obviously still alive and well. Emily had rescued him from a gang who were ill-treating him when he was a tiny kitten. She'd snatching him up, ignoring the taunts of the teenage boys, wrapped him in her cardigan and carried him back to Laurel Terrace.

The door creaked open and Ada peered up at her through a thatch of hair as unruly as Emily's own – except that Ada's was silver and Emily's was a mass of crow-black curls. Their eyes were the same – described by Ada's husband Frank as being like liquid amber.

"I thought you'd be back," said Ada when they were sitting in the garden with a pot of tea and some of her cinnamon toast. "Couldn't imagine you staying away for too long."

Emily felt she wouldn't be able to eat anything, despite her stomach growling with hunger, but Ada had waved away her protests telling her that everything would seem better once she'd eaten something.

The scent of sweet peas and honeysuckle surrounded them and Emily began to relax for the first time in several days. Nelson climbed on her lap and settled there, for once not digging his claws in, as if he knew she needed looking after.

"He remembers you," said Ada sipping her tea. "You wouldn't think, looking at him now, that yesterday he had a go at the postman, the milkman and the lady who came to read the gas meter."

They sat in silence for a while.

"So what happened?" asked Ada looking remarkably alert for someone of ninety. "I had a feeling London wasn't the right place for you. There seemed no point in paying good money to that college to learn what you knew already – and I didn't like the look of that bloke you'd taken up with. His eyes were too close together." She took a sip of tea. "Mind you, when you were a little girl I felt sure you'd end up running one of them animal sanctuaries, the number of waifs and strays you brought back here."

Emily sat staring at her hands – for once clean and not spattered with paint. She felt touched at Ada's belief in her but it didn't take away the pain of her failed venture – and betrayal by the person she thought loved her.

"Everything went wrong," said Emily. "I made a stupid mistake, I've lost everything and I don't think I'll ever paint again."

"Fish-hooks and rhubarb," said Ada. "Of course you will. You'll survive this and come back even stronger just like I did." She picked up the tea tray and went indoors to make them scrambled eggs for tea, leaving Emily to wonder what problems her Gran, who'd lived all her life in Laurel Terrace, could possibly have overcome.

There had only been one occasion when Emily was staying with her and Granddad one summer holiday after her Mum and Dad split up that anything had been said to make her think otherwise.

"Did you always want to marry Granny Ada?" she'd asked Granddad Frank one day while they were in the garden picking sweet peas.

"You bet," he'd said with a grin. "Not so sure about her though. I was always her Second Best Boy."

Gran, bringing a tray of cold drinks into the garden, had silenced him with a look.

Later, when Emily was in her old bedroom with its dark oak furniture and red and gold satin bedspread, she gave vent to the tears that she'd been holding back all day. She'd gone to London with such high expectations – of becoming a well-known artist, meeting someone special and eventually settling in a country cottage with dogs and children and her own art studio.

It had gone well to start with – she'd finished her course and the comments about her work had been favourable. Then a year ago, on the first day of an exhibition in a gallery in Chelsea, she'd met James. She'd gone outside for a breath of air – it had been a stiflingly hot day in London. She was wearing a pink lace dress that showed off her slim figure and her mop of dark curls was pinned on top of her head. He'd smiled at her, she'd noticed how his eyes were green flecked with gold like the sun on a summer sea under neatly trimmed fair hair.

He was wearing dark trousers and a crisp white shirt with the sleeves rolled back. She noticed, with an artist's eye, how the coppery hairs on his arms glinted in the sunlight.

He followed her into the gallery, accepted a glass of champagne and promptly bought one of her paintings. They chatted until the gallery closed and it was as if she'd known him years.

The following day, to the gallery owner's amusement, he was back again. This time he insisted on taking her to dinner after closing time, stopping at a florist's to buy her a dozen foxglove pink roses that matched the colour of her dress.

They'd gone to a bistro with tables outside and eaten lasagne with red wine. He'd walked her back to her flat and kissed her goodnight. It was a warm starlit night and everything in her life felt perfect.

Thinking back, she should've been suspicious because in all the time they were together she'd never met his family, friends or work-mates.

*"I don't want to share you with anyone,"* he'd said. *"You're too precious."*

He told her he worked in finance – and he certainly looked the part with his smart suits and crisp white shirts. He was romantic but never pushy, took her to quiet, romantic places but didn't intrude too much on the time she needed for her work.

Emily had originally thought she'd need to move out of London once she finished her course. She'd looked at little galleries to rent in places like Oxford and Brighton and spent ages scribbling figures on pieces of paper wondering whether she could make a living from her artwork. She'd discussed this with James and he'd listened when she'd told him how much she'd saved. Since she was a child she'd dreamed of owning her own gallery and art studio.

One evening, James had taken her on what he called a 'mystery tour.' He insisted she closed her eyes and then led her down a street where spicy aromas and the smell of strong coffee drifted through open doorways on a babble of music and chatter.

He unlocked a door, led her through it into a space that felt cool on her bare arms after the warmth outside. He told her to open her eyes and she found herself in a small white-washed room.

"Your new gallery," he said. "What are we going to call it?"

Emily got out of bed and paced restlessly around the room. She looked through the curtains at the pathway of moonlight across the garden. When she and Angie were children they once made wishes on a moonlit night like this. Gran and Angie's Auntie Molly had let them go out in their night clothes and it had seemed like a magical adventure. Angie's dream was to run her own café. Well, from the sound of it she'd succeeded where Emily had failed because she'd made the mistake of trusting someone who said he loved her.

Emily pulled the curtains back, opened the window and leaned out watching moths drift ghost-like around purple clematis flowers, silvered in the moonlight.

She'd had her dream – Gallery Emily – for such a short time. It was her own fault. She'd not questioned anything when James presented her with a contract in her name, produced a pen and asked her to sign it. He'd said he loved her. She trusted him. She hadn't even read the contract. She'd handed over the money for the first three months' rent. It seemed a huge amount but James assured her the price was fair. He'd pocketed the money, kissed her and they'd gone to a bistro down a quiet street to celebrate.

Emily remembered how excited she'd been handing out the black and gold business cards that matched the sign that hung over the door 'Gallery Emily.'

It hurt to think how much he must have been laughing at her, how young and gullible she must have seemed.

There had been the magic of the opening night when all her old college friends had come, casting envious glances as they drank her champagne and ate the delicious nibbles she'd spent ages preparing. Soft music had played and after everyone had gone, James had poured more champagne for her and danced with her amongst the spot-lit canvases.

It was strange, thinking back, that none of his friends or contacts had come.

As time went on, some weeks she didn't see him much. He was busy with work, he said. He had to do a lot of travelling for meetings. Emily used the time they were apart to paint furiously. She experimented with different ideas – working from meditations to create dream-like pictures and mixing aromatherapy oils with the paint.

Her customers said that a visit to her gallery was like a 'feast for the senses.' Not only did they have beautiful paintings to look at, but there was soft music, seats with velvet and satin cushions, the scent of rose and lavender mixed with fresh coffee and a tempting array of bite sized cakes.

There was a wonderful space at the back of the gallery like a lean-to with a glass roof that provided good light but was icy cold in winter however much heating she put on. She painted muffled up in hat, scarf and fingerless mittens: *"My little Eskimo,"* he'd called her, kissing the tip of her cold nose when he called in to visit one day.

He took an interest in how much she was selling. He said he'd handle the business side so she could just paint and not worry. Her work sold well. Emily handed over the money for her sales as well as the next three months' rent. She wondered now why she'd never thought to ask for receipts – or why he as a businessman had never offered them to her.

Then last Tuesday – a day of Mediterranean blue sky and sunshine, she arrived at the gallery early. She'd stopped at the deli to buy *pain au chocolat* for her breakfast and a latte and was looking forward to finishing a painting of a mermaid ordered by one of the local cafes.

A woman with short brown hair and red lipstick dressed in jeans and a crumpled linen blouse was waiting outside the gallery.

"Where is he?" she asked.

"Where's who?" asked Emily whose mind had been on the mermaid picture.

"My husband."

Emily wondered if the woman was slightly mad – or if she'd had too much sun.

"Jay, Jamie, James," whatever name he's using at the moment."

"My boyfriend's called James," said Emily.

"Well, where is he? He's done it again and I'm not standing for it this time."

"Done what? You'd better come in. None of this makes any sense." Emily opened the door and they went into the gallery. The woman sat down on one of Emily's red velvet sofas and looked about her as if waiting for something.

Emily remembered her coffee and *pain au chocolat.* "We could share this," she said going out into her small kitchen and pouring the coffee into two mugs.

"Nice place," said the woman when Emily returned. "I wondered what it would be this time. Over the last few years it's been a hairdressers, a dress shop, a florist, a shoe shop, a café…" She ticked the places off on her fingers.

Emily wondered what any of this had to do with her.

Then a few minutes later a man in a grey suit walked into the gallery.

"I presume you're Miss Randall," he said looking Emily up and down. "I'm Geoff Price, your landlord. "I'm just wondering if you've got the money yet for your last three months' rent."

Emily felt as if someone had just thrown a bucket of cold water over her.

"But I've paid it," she said.

"Prove it," he said, a nasty smile on his face.

"I gave the money to James – Mr Alexander – for him to pass on to you," said Emily.

"I've heard that one before," said the landlord. "You'd better come up with a better excuse than that, Miss Randall, or I'll be seeing you in court."

"Mr Alexander is the one you should be taking to court," said the woman getting to her feet, "and I'll be the first in the queue. He owes me big time."

"And who might you be?" The landlord frowned at her suspiciously.

"I'm Claire Alexander, James's wife and the mother of his children. As you well know, this young woman isn't the only one to be taken in by the pair of you. You've got a good scam going between you. Well, not anymore." She turned to Emily. "Go home to your mother, dear. I'll sort this out."

Emily stared at the pair of them. None of this made any sense. The coffee and *pain au chocolat* she'd just eaten was making her feel queasy. With a sense of relief she saw James crossing the street towards the gallery. He'd be able to sort out the muddle. She felt as if she'd woken up in the middle of a dark fairy-tale.

James walked straight in and took Emily in his arms. He didn't notice Claire and the landlord who were in shadow. "You look beautiful today," he said.

"You used to say that to me once," said Claire rising to her feet, "before you got taken over by gambling."

Events happened in slow motion after that. All Emily could remember was gathering as many of her possessions as she could carry away from the gallery and hurrying in the direction of her flat. She managed to get to the safety of her room before grief and shock overwhelmed her and she lay in bed for two days unable to do anything but cry.

Her flatmates urged her to go to Citizen's Advice. She did so but was told that without proof of handing over any money, she hadn't a leg to stand on. James had helped her set up a bank account and she'd left it to him to pay any cheques in. He'd given her cash for her living expenses. She'd trusted him completely. Now she couldn't believe how stupid she'd been. There was no way of proving anything.

When Emily and her flatmates went to the gallery everything had been stripped out and all her signs removed. It looked just as it did the first time she saw it

– like a blank canvas. If it hadn't been for the photos she'd taken she could easily believe it had all been a dream.

There was nothing to stay in London for now – and anyway she couldn't afford it now her means of earning a living and most of her savings were gone. Her completed artwork had all been in the gallery and had no doubt been sold by now. She couldn't face the thought of starting all over again.

Emily craved green fields and woodland and a place to lick her wounds in peace. She had no idea what she'd do with her life now that all she'd ever wanted had been so cruelly snatched away.

A week later, she packed up her things and headed for Paddington Station and the train back to Marchwood.

Ada Brookes was also awake during the night. She knew what it was like to have your life turned suddenly upside down. She gave thanks that Frank had been there for her as friend when she'd needed one – and that they'd had a good life together even if it wasn't the one she originally planned.

He'd called round as soon as he'd heard the news about Jack, still in his railway uniform, smelling faintly of coal and sweat, twisting his cap awkwardly in his big work-red hands that were so different from Jack's long slim ones. He was quick to reassure her that the planned elopement wasn't common knowledge – and that her secret was safe with him.

Ada's mother told her to invite him Frank in for a cup of tea.

"I don't hold with gossiping on the door-step," she said. "The neighbours'll talk."

After he'd gone, she said: "I'd have thought with your looks Ada you'd have set your sights a bit higher than a railway porter – but as long as you're happy that's all that matters."

Ada didn't say anything. She was thankful her mother didn't realise how close things had come to Ada really giving the neighbours something to talk about.

She left the box with the ruby necklace where it was. She didn't even tell Frank about it. It was her secret, the only reminder she'd got of Jack, apart from the article about him that she'd cut carefully out of the newspaper and kept in the box in her dressing table that held her Sunday School certificates and the pearl necklace she'd inherited from her godmother.

When she and Frank married the following year, she was happy with the simple topaz and marcasite ring he bought her from an antique shop because he said the colour reminded him of her eyes.

Emily and Ada sat at the breakfast table the next morning both looking as if they'd had a sleepless night. They drank tea and ate toast and marmalade. Ada was very definite that nobody left her house in the morning without having breakfast first.

"You might find second best is better in the long run," Ada said when Emily kissed her goodbye, saying she was going into Marchwood to sign on with an Agency.

She looked as if she was going to say more, but she was interrupted by the arrival of the postman and needed to go and protect him from Nelson.

Emily walked past the overgrown front gardens of Laurel Terrace feeling strange and out of place. When she was a child, the area had been a hive of activity with the factories that had produced everything from children's clothes to garden ornaments. The smell of meat and onion pies hung over the area making Emily and Angie feel hungry for their lunch when they were playing outside in one of their gardens.

Now all Emily could smell was traffic fumes as she headed into Marchwood town centre past the entrance to the park where Angie said her new café was. It was painted bright pink and Angie said 'you couldn't miss it.'

Emily had agonised over what to wear and eventually decided on her best jeans and a cream silk blouse. She didn't own anything that could be described as 'office dress.'

In the finish when she got to the agency, it wouldn't have mattered if she'd been in pyjamas. The place was in chaos. There were three desks that had unopened post on them and one lady with frizzy ginger hair, a harassed expression and a badge that said 'Glenda – here to help' trying to answer phones that didn't stop ringing.

Emily stepped in and helped, copying what the woman said by way of introduction but substituting her own name. *"Good morning. Premier Recruitment. Emily speaking. How can I help you?"* earning a grateful smile from Glenda.

Two hours later, she walked out of there with a job to start the following day.

Something about the name 'Richard Kingsley Associates' sounded familiar but she couldn't think why.

"He lives in that big house with the wall round it near the church," said Glenda at the Agency. "His wife died in a car accident a couple of years ago."

Back at Laurel Terrace, over tea and slices of lemon drizzle cake in the garden, Emily told Ada about her new job and asked if she knew anything about the family.

"No – I don't know anything about them," Ada said, but Emily noticed how her face drained of colour and that she quickly changed the subject.

Later, Ada wondered why she hadn't told Emily about Jack. After all, it happened seventy years ago, Frank was dead, she wasn't getting any younger and she didn't want the secret to die with her.

# CHAPTER TWO

June 2016

Richard Llewellyn Kingsley was sure he'd walked into the wrong office. Then he remembered his secretary, Monica, was having a hysterectomy.

The waif-like girl sitting crossed-legged on the floor was wearing layers of black net with a strappy top that looked more suitable for a nightclub. Her cloud of curly dark hair rippled over her shoulders in direct contrast to Monica's neat French plait. Her eyes were closed.

Richard sighed. He had an important meeting in an hour's time about the designs he'd proposed for the library reading room at a university in Munich. It involved a glass dome that allowed light to flood in and marble steps that gave an impression of water flowing. The designs had been well-received at first, but now the finance people had got hold of it and wanted corners to be cut and economies made. The project was important because it would make a significant amount of money that would help to offset his financial problems.

The new girl was showing more flesh than a butcher's shop and there was a strong smell of incense that didn't create the right impression.

He cleared his throat.

The girl opened eyes like pools of liquid amber. "I'm not late am I? I got here early so I could calm down a bit."

Richard felt himself going hot. He'd definitely be finished if the people arrived for the meeting early and walked in on a scene that looked like something out of 'Fifty Shades of Grey.'

"We have a meeting in less than an hour," he said briskly.

She opened her eyes wide. "I know, it's in the diary."

Richard cleared his throat again. "I trust you'll be changing into something more –suitable - to take the minutes?"

"The agency didn't say anything about taking minutes – and …" she looked crestfallen. "This is my best outfit. I haven't got anything else."

Richard got out his wallet. "There's a dress shop just along the road. See if you can find something less… revealing. And we'll need milk for the coffee. There doesn't appear to be any." The efficient Monica would, of course, have cleared the fridge before she left for her cancellation appointment.

Richard handed over three twenty pound notes.

The girl took off like a greyhound and Richard wondered fleetingly if he'd see her or his money again. He opened the window to dispel the scent of patchouli. Then he went to Monica's desk drawer. He was thankful to notice the paperwork for the meeting was printed and neatly stapled.

The girl came back loaded with carrier bags and hurried into the kitchen. She emerged a few minutes later wearing a damson coloured lace dress that at least covered her arms and some of her chest even if it barely covered her knickers.

"It's a bit short isn't it?"

She pulled a funny face at him. "I've bought some black tights."

She busied herself adding slices of orange to the jugs of water.

"Monica uses lemon."

"I'm not Monica – I'm Emily and I think orange is nicer."

She handed him back two of the twenty pound notes.

"You came back with enough bags – it must have cost more than twenty pounds, surely?"

Lacey – the girl he'd met on his recent stay in America would've spent the full amount without blinking.

"Charity shops are great aren't they? You never know what you might find "

"I don't know, I've never been in one."

The girl couldn't have looked more surprised if he'd said he'd just landed from Mars.

"They said at the agency that you're loaded. I don't suppose you have to buy the nearly out of date stuff in supermarkets either like I did when I was a student."

The phone rang and Richard was saved from having to admit that he'd never had much to do with supermarkets either. He had a housekeeper who organised the grocery shopping. By the time he'd finished the call, Emily had added tights and burgundy velvet shoes to her new outfit and had tidied her unruly mane of hair into a single plait. There were plates of sliced fruit on the table – melon, strawberries and pineapple – alongside the chocolate digestives left by Monica.

Before Richard had time to say anything, the clamour of voices in the foyer announced that the people attending the meeting had arrived. The receptionist led them through to the meeting room where Emily was busy pouring coffee.

"Hey Richard, things are looking up," said one of the men, digging him in the ribs as he took in both Emily and the plates of fruit. "Monica will have to watch her step."

Richard wasn't so sure about that, although as the meeting progressed, he had to admit Emily played her part well. She smiled in all the right places, served the coffee without spilling it and appeared to be coping with the minutes. The problem was getting the finance guys to agree and from the look on their faces and the comments they made, this was looking doubtful.

Richard tried not to look or sound desperate but his heart was sinking further with every argument they came up with about changing the design of the steps or economising on the glass used for the dome. There was even talk of postponing the project for two years.

Richard's financial advisor had been pushing him to find ways of generating more income in order to offset the debts left by his father who had died recently. It seemed that every time Andrew Crane got in touch with him, it was to spin another tale of woe and potential loss.

He knew his creditors had been more than lenient already following the sudden death of his wife, Helen, in an accident leaving him unable to sort things out. Richard had taken the escape route offered to him and gone to America on a short-term work contract, leaving his little daughter Julia in the care of his sister Thea. Over there, he'd felt different and could almost feel that the events of the previous year hadn't happened. Then an urgent call from his financial advisor, Andrew Crane, had brought him home. It was time to face up to his problems. At the moment he was praying for a miracle that would enable him to keep Oakwood House, the home that had been in his family for two hundred years. He had three months to come up with a viable plan to pay off the outstanding debts. If they could not do this, then Richard would have to sell his beloved house.

Richard sat feeling as if his head was full of cotton wool. The words dropped like stones around him. He just wanted the meeting to be over. From the look on the faces around the table he felt he was fighting a lost cause.

They'd got to Any Other Business on the agenda when one of the women let out a shriek. "Something just touched my leg. You have rats here?" She leapt onto her chair.

Emily turned pale and was out of her seat and under the table, providing the group with a view of her shapely legs and bottom.

When she stood up, she was cradling a black and white lop-eared rabbit, a defiant expression on her face.

"I had to buy him," she said. "The pet shop down the road is closing down. He'd have been put to sleep if I hadn't taken him."

The meeting had ended in disarray with the women gathering round to make a fuss of the rabbit as if it was a new baby.

"I'm so sorry," Emily burst out as soon as everyone had gone. "Rufus wouldn't stay in his box. I didn't mean for that to happen. I hope it didn't mess things up for you."

She looked as if she was about to cry – something Richard knew he didn't cope well with.

"Don't worry about it – you and the rabbit couldn't have made things any worse." His head ached and he just wanted to be on his own.

She stood there holding the rabbit in her arms, reminding him of his first sight of his wife Helen cradling their new-born daughter Julia. The memory brought a lump to his throat.

"You'd better go and get a hutch for that creature or you'll get no work done this afternoon either," he said gruffly. "Get the Receptionist to keep an eye on it while you nip down to the shop."

He handed over forty pounds and she sped off. He caught a glance at the rabbit, sitting in a cardboard box on the Reception desk nibbling a carrot. It looked smug.

By five o'clock it was raining – huge drops lashed the windows and grey cloud hung over the town like a woolly hat. Richard noticed Emily struggling towards the stairs with the cage in her arms, her handbag and two canvas bags slung over her right shoulder. One bag contained straw, rabbit food and a water bottle, the other contained the clothes she was wearing this morning.

"Where's your car parked?" he asked taking the hutch off her.

"I haven't got one at the moment." She looked more waif-like than usual with all her belongings.

"Getting a taxi home, are you?"

She turned huge amber eyes on him. "I wish! I don't get paid till Friday."

"But it's raining."

"So I'll get wet, won't I?"

"Where do you live?"

"Laurel Terrace – on the other side of town near the station and the old factories."

Richard knew the area. It had been in decline since the last of the factories closed and there was talk of pulling most of it down and creating some upmarket apartments, shops and restaurants.

"How will you get there?"

"Walk. I left my roller skates at home." She smiled to soften the sarcasm and the colour of her eyes reminded him of sunlight on a jar of dark honey.

As he followed her down the stairs, Richard knew the sensible thing would be to give her money for a taxi. He almost couldn't believe it when he heard himself say: "You can't do that. I'll give you a lift."

"But you're not going that way?"

"How do you know?" It was his turn to stare back at her.

"Glenda at the Agency told me where you live."

Richard felt as if his collar was too tight. He wondered what other titbits about his life Glenda at the Agency had been spreading around. "Come on then if you're taking up my offer. Let's get out of the rain." He spoke more sharply than he intended.

He led the way to his car and opened the boot but Emily looked horrified. "He'll suffocate in there. He needs to go on the back seat."

Richard felt stressed at the thought of the pristine perfection of the black leather interior of his BMW being damaged. It was one of the few things he had any control over at the moment and as always when he was stressed he went a bit over the top with it. He got the tartan picnic blanket out of the boot and laid it on the back seat, hoping that the rough wooden corners of the hutch wouldn't scratch the leather through it.

He tried not to think about sawdust and worse going all over the floor as he settled the rabbit in, opened the front passenger door for Emily, started the engine and edged his way into the stream of traffic passing through the town centre.

His sister had always teased him about what she called his OCD traits. When they were children, she was the one who came back covered in mud. Richard was the one who could be relied on to stay clean and tidy. Thea's room was always like a jumble sale, whereas Richard's toys were neatly put away.

That was the thing he most liked when he first met Lacey – the fact that she understood his need for order. Her apartment overlooking Boston Harbour was the epitome of good taste and he'd drifted into an easy relationship with her where she sorted out what they were doing and he just followed. Looking back, he realised he'd drifted through his time in America on autopilot.

It was only when he returned to England that he realised how close he'd come to marrying Lacey on the rebound. There had been the night just before he got the phone call from Andrew Crane summoning him home when they'd gone out for a meal in Boston. They'd gone back to her apartment and stood by the window looking out at the pathway of stars above the harbour. An old-fashioned sailing ship in full sail was riding at anchor adding to the romantic atmosphere. She'd turned to him and he'd kissed her. When they broke away from each other, he'd been on the point of proposing. In the fraction of a second it took to frame the question, someone rang the doorbell of the apartment and the moment was lost.

Richard looked at Emily sitting beside him. She was as different from Lacey as chalk and cheese. Lacey wasn't the sort of person to rescue a rabbit or any other living creature. She dealt briskly with any moths or spiders who strayed into the pristine whiteness of her apartment and was harshly critical of any of her friends who plastered their Facebook pages with photos of cute kittens and puppies.

Richard's heart sank. The incident at the meeting had probably been widely reported by now and Rufus the rabbit probably had his own Facebook fan club by now.

"Where would you like me to drop you off?" he asked when he reached the road that led to Laurel Terrace.

"Just there on the right please," she said pointing to a row of terraced houses most of which looked as if they were about to be swallowed by overgrown bushes. "Second one in."

Richard helped her lift the hutch off the back seat. He was thankful to see that, apart from a scattering of sawdust, there was no major damage to the interior of his car.

"Thank you so much for bringing us home," she said, her amber eyes brimming. "I'll work extra hard tomorrow."

Richard headed back to Oakwood House. After he'd gone through the electronic gates the narrow road wound up through an avenue of copper beeches opening out onto a carriage ring in front of the square white Georgian house.

He let himself in through the front door into the black and white tiled entrance hall with its cut glass chandelier and stood gazing around wondering how much longer he'd be able to keep the house.

Joshua Kingsley had founded the family's fortunes in the early 1800s by working for the East India Company. He'd built Oakwood House in 1815, the year of Waterloo. Large portraits of a grim looking Joshua and his beautiful wife Elizabeth hung on either side of the marble fireplace. Elizabeth was wearing the filigree silver and ruby necklace that had once belonged to an Indian rajah.

The smell of beef casserole drifted along the passageway from the kitchen. Ginny, his housekeeper, greeted him on her way to the dining room to lay the table for him. Dinner would be ready in half an hour.

Richard went up the curved staircase to his bedroom, remembering how he and Thea used to slide down the polished wooden bannisters when they were children. It wasn't until he looked at the calendar on his bedside table that he realised the significance of the date. It would've been Helen's thirtieth birthday today. They'd had so little time together. He sat on the bed as daylight faded outside the long sash windows trying to remember her face and the texture of her blonde hair but found that it was lost in a sort of mist.

The only face that came to mind wasn't Helen's, the woman he expected to love forever. It had amber eyes surrounded by wild black hair.

## CHAPTER THREE

June 2016

"Was that you getting out of a posh car?" Ada asked Emily when she staggered in through the front door with Rufus in his hutch. "Where did you get that rabbit?"

"Richard Kingsley gave me a lift home from work," said Emily feeling a blush rise to her cheeks. "It was raining and he didn't want me walking home with all my stuff."

"You watch yourself young lady. I've heard those Kingsley men can be very charming."

"I'm not going out with him or anything," said Emily hotly. "I'm surprised he offered me a lift, I've caused him nothing but trouble all day. And anyway – Glenda at the Agency said his wife died a couple of years ago so he's probably not interested in finding anyone else right now."

At that moment Nelson rushed in from the garden, ginger fur bristling. He circled round Emily and then attempted to climb up her legs, hissing angrily, his yellow eye sparking golden fire.

"Stop it Nelson," said Emily, "these are new tights."

"New dress as well by the look of it," said Ada going out to the kitchen to put the kettle on. "Where did that come from?" The smell of freshly baked jam tarts hung in the warm air. Ada's new mission in life was to make sure Emily didn't starve.

"Mr Kingsley said I wasn't dressed smartly enough for his meeting," said Emily. "He gave me the money to go and get something more suitable. I went to the charity shop."

"So were they giving away rabbits with each purchase?" asked Ada pouring the tea.

"Funny," said Emily with a smile. "The pet shop was closing down and Rufus was going to be put to sleep. I just couldn't let that happen."

Emily had put Rufus in his hutch on the worktop in the scullery. She'd shut the door to keep Nelson out but he was sat there his fur bristling and tail swishing. He glared at Emily as if she was a traitor.

"I still love you best Nelson," said Emily biting into a jam tart. "I just couldn't leave Rufus where he was because the pet shop was closing down and they'd have had him put to sleep." Nelson didn't look impressed. He turned his back on Emily.

"You never could resist a story like that, could you?" said Ada with a gentle smile.

"No, I couldn't could I?" said Emily, feeling suddenly not hungry any more as she thought of James and the way she'd been deceived.

By the time they'd washed up after tea – Ada had treated them to fish and chips – it was clear that it wasn't going to be possible to keep Rufus. Nelson was clawing at the door eager to get at his enemy.

"The landlord's coming tomorrow to do an inspection," said Ada, "and you know what he's like about no pets being allowed. I just hope he doesn't ask any questions about the way Nelson's scratched at that door. Nelson's a sensible cat – he usually has the sense to stay out of the way if he's around and I always hide his food bowls and the cat food.

"I'll take Rufus with me tomorrow," said Emily. "When I get to work I can phone round some of the rescue centres and see if they'll take him. I can balance him on that old pram you use for shopping."

"You mind you bring it back then," said Ada. "I'm hoping I live long enough to push at least one of your babies in it."

"You've got more chance of having one yourself," said Emily with a smile. However, as she got up to put the kettle on to make tea a memory of Richard's sea-green eyes came into her mind and the texture of his wavy treacle-toffee coloured hair.

*"He's not interested in you,"* she told herself. *"He was just trying to impress those visitors."*

That evening after dinner, Richard had a phone call from his sister Thea. He was sitting in what used to be their father's gun room but was now furnished as a cosy study for him with dark green walls and a sturdy leather-topped oak desk. A fire burned in the grate during the winter, but at the moment the fireplace was stacked with an arrangement of pine cones. Photos of him and Thea when they were children were on the desk – both in jeans and sweaters with tangled hair and faces streaked with mud.

Thea was two years younger than him and through their childhood they had been constant companions, exploring, climbing trees and riding their bikes together. Thea had married first and now lived in rural Herefordshire with her husband, three little boys and two black Labradors.

It was Thea who had seen through the brave face Richard had put on following the death of their father, rapidly followed by the death of his wife Helen in a car accident one foggy November night. They knew their father hadn't left his affairs in very good order but the extent of the mismanagement wasn't known at the time.

Richard had struggled to cope with four year old Julia who was so much like her mother it almost hurt him to look at her. Julia had been told her Mummy was in Heaven and occupied her time creating endless pictures for her to see when she came back. Richard couldn't find the words to tell her that her beloved mother would never return.

It was Thea who had arrived at Oakwood House, summoned by an anxious Ginny, to find that Richard, who'd been struggling to come to terms with his grief, couldn't summon the energy to get out of bed and dress, let alone look after his daughter. She'd talked him into seeing the doctor who had prescribed antidepressants and a change of scene. Just after that, a temporary contract in America had come up and Thea had urged him to take it, saying she would look after Julia as a temporary measure.

By the time the arrangements were made, Helen had been dead for over a year. The contract was supposed to be for three months but had stretched to six, only ending when the financial advisor sorting out their father's affairs had contacted Richard to warn him about how bad things were.

Thea had their mother's colouring – auburn hair and brown eyes. She was practical and down to earth and had been meticulous in keeping Richard up to date with Julia's health and progress. She always had a reason for getting in touch with him and he wondered with a tremor of unease what the problem was.

As always, Thea was direct and to the point. "I'm calling to invite you to lunch on Sunday. Adam has been offered a temporary promotion – the only problem is it's in Edinburgh – and I feel it's only right that you should have Julia back with you now."

Richard gulped. His utter sense of failure where looking after his daughter was concerned swamped him like a tidal wave. It was bad enough looking at her photo without having the real-life version mirroring Helen's mannerisms and facial expressions.

"I'm not sure I can," he said. "I wasn't much good at it before."

"You wouldn't be on your own," said Thea soothingly. "I've spoken to Ginny about finding a nanny and she thinks she knows just the person."

"So you've been talking about me behind my back," said Richard. "No change there then."

"Right in one," said Thea.

"I just wish Dad's affairs could be sorted as easily."

"You mean – a miracle like finding the Rajah's necklace?"

"Yes – and the other stuff that went missing during the last war. Andrew Crane the financial guy has checked all the inventories and has come up with loads of stuff that doesn't seem to be here anymore. It's almost as if he thinks I've stashed it somewhere."

"Is it – very serious?" There was a catch in Thea's voice.

"Yes." There was no point pretending otherwise with her. She'd always detect a lie. "I – we - could lose the house and have to move somewhere else. I just can't imagine living anywhere else on a permanent basis."

"Don't go getting yourself stressed again," said Thea. "We'll have a chat about possible options on Sunday."

Richard knew she was only trying to help – and he knew she was afraid of him descending into the depression he'd been in after Helen died. He tried not to sound dismissive but he didn't think there was anything they could come up with that would provide enough money to keep Oakwood House in the family.

He put the phone down. His head was pounding and he felt drained and tired. He looked at the black and white studio photo of Helen and Julia on top of the bookcase. He wondered how he'd cope with having Julia with him – a constant reminder of the wife he'd loved and lost.

His mobile bleeped with an incoming text. Richard checked his phone – something he was notoriously bad at doing. Unlike most people on the planet, he found mobile phones intrusive and had as little to do with his as possible.

To his surprise, he had several missed calls from Lacey, the girl he'd met in Boston.

*"Really missing you sweetie."*

*"Wish you were here with me. The nights are too long without you."*

*"I so miss hearing your voice."*

*"Please call me. I need to talk to you. We have unfinished business."*

Richard felt uneasy, wondering what she meant by 'unfinished business.' His emotions were still fragile at times. He hoped he hadn't given her the wrong impression about his feelings for her. He definitely wasn't ready to make a firm commitment to anyone at the moment.

He looked back at the photo of his wife and daughter. No – his heart wasn't ready to move on yet.

# CHAPTER FOUR

## June 2016

Emily got up early to make sure Rufus and Nelson were out of the house before the landlord arrived. She'd taken Ada a cup of tea in bed, and was pleased to see her grandmother's room hadn't changed.

It still had the familiar cornflower patterned wallpaper and the red, white and blue patchwork quilt that had been made by Ada's mother for the coronation of Edward VII when the houses in Laurel Terrace were still considered 'new.' The bed was the familiar double one with the black wrought iron roses at the head and foot that Emily had enjoyed running her finger round when she was a child.

"Those factories and their smoke used to play havoc with my mother's clean sheets," Ada once said. "She was always complaining about it."

Now, of course, none of the factories were working and many of the houses in Laurel Terrace that once housed some of the workers stood empty.

"You have made sure to eat some breakfast haven't you?" Ada asked.

"Yes," said Emily. In reality she hadn't been able to eat more than a few mouthfuls of cereal. She'd been plagued by another sleepless night when images of James's betrayal had run in an endless loop through her mind.

Last night she'd looked at the glossy leaflet Angie had pushed into one of her bags. Emily had felt the familiar stab of envy that her friend appeared to have achieved the success that had been snatched from her so cruelly.

She knew, of course, that things hadn't been plain sailing for Angie. Ada had kept her updated as to Angie's progress from buying a 'snack caravan' and selling bacon sandwiches and mugs of tea in a lay-by with a friend of hers from catering college.

She'd progressed from this to several tiny cafes and now 'Angie's Café' – complete with pink and gold sign had opened near the tennis courts in Marchwood Park. The leaflet promised that future attractions would include a pet's corner for children and craft events.

Emily had tried to phone Angie to ask if she'd fancy trying out the pet's corner for the day with Rufus – but the phone had just switched to voice mail. However, she decided as she was leaving early that morning she could walk the long way round through the park and see. Failing that, she would plead with the pet shop to keep him just for the day. Either way, when she got to work she'd phone some animal sanctuaries and vets and see if there was anyone who would look after Rufus and love him.

"Don't forget to put Nelson's bowls away under the sink," said Ada. "And spray some of that lily of the valley air freshener to cover up the smell of cat food. That landlord's got a nose like a bloodhound."

A yowl and a thump from downstairs was Nelson's way of telling them both that he didn't think much of Rufus.

"I'd better go," said Emily kissing her grandmother goodbye.

Nelson glared balefully at Emily when she pushed him outside into the garden. Rufus carried on eating his dried food, his facial expression bordering on what might be called 'dumb insolence' as he stared back at Nelson. Emily felt a stab of envy that nothing seemed to worry him.

Emily arrived at work feeling as if she'd already completed a marathon. There was nobody at the café. She'd attracted a few smiles and curious glances as she'd walked through the park pushing the big navy blue pram with Rufus's hutch strapped on top of it. Big pink and gold signs advertised the current special offers and Emily felt a stab of sorrow when she remembered the opening night of her own gallery.

She turned away from the café and headed along the pathway that led into town, swallowing down the threatened tears.

The people in the pet shop where she'd bought Rufus were in the process of clearing out their last bits and pieces of stock. They were also moving out of the flat above the shop so the place was also piled with furniture, bedding and bin bags full of clothes.

"Sorry love, can't help you," the lady said. "We're not planning to be here longer than a couple of hours."

From the look of the massive amount of stuff that needed to be cleared, two weeks seemed more likely. It was clear from their attitude they didn't expect her to come back for him.

Emily didn't feel like pleading with them.

The receptionist at the vet's was more helpful. She did at least give Emily the phone numbers of a few rescue centres.

"So what do we do with you?" Emily asked Rufus. Her feet ached and she desperately needed a cup of tea.

Rufus twitched his whiskers and nibbled a piece of carrot.

A quick check of the car park revealed that Richard hadn't arrived at work yet. Emily also remembered that the receptionist wasn't in either that day. She unstrapped the hutch and pushed the pram into the space round the back of the building where the bins were kept. It was bin day yesterday so hopefully it would be safe – Ada would have something to say if Emily came home without the pram.

She carried Rufus and her bag up the stairs and put him under the table in the kitchen. She put a cloth on the table that hung down, hiding him from view.

Before Richard got into work, Emily phoned two of the animal charities on the list. Neither switchboard was answering so she left messages, asking them to say it was a personal call when they got back to her.

She made herself a cup of tea and nibbled a biscuit. At that moment Richard arrived.

She made coffee for him and took it into his office. He looked as if he'd had the same sort of night as she had and then she remembered about his wife and thought how much worse that must be than the situation she was in. The phone rang almost as soon as she left his office and she tensed, thinking it was one of the animal charities calling back.

It wasn't, so she went back to her desk and tried to get on with the work she'd been asked to do.

By lunchtime neither of the charities had called back. Emily realised she needed to get some greens for Rufus and also some lunch for herself. Her stomach was churning in an alarming fashion and she began to feel light-headed. Richard was on the phone and his door was firmly shut.

The market was only five minutes' walk away. The lady at the pet shop had told her there was a bin used by the fruit and veg stalls where they disposed of the outer leaves and stalks. They didn't mind people helping themselves as long as they took their own bags. She could collect food for Rufus and a sandwich for herself from the cheap supermarket on the corner.

It was only when she got to the supermarket that she realised she had no money in her purse. Feeling flustered, she left the queue, put the sandwich back in the chiller cabinet and headed back to the office with the bag of greens. She'd have to make do with more biscuits and any left-over fruit from the meeting yesterday.

However, when she got into the kitchen, intending to stash the bag of greens under the table beside the hutch, Richard was there with a face like thunder. The cloth was off the table and Rufus was in full view.

"What on earth's going on? You're turning this place into a circus. I gave you the money yesterday for a hutch for that creature. What's he doing back here today?"

In the middle of Emily's tearful apology and garbled explanation about the landlord not wanting pets, the phone rang.

"Wonderful," snapped Richard snatching up the phone. "How am I supposed to get any work done when this thing keeps ringing all day?"

He stomped off to his office and slammed the door leaving Emily unsure what to do next.

"I hope I wasn't interrupting anything important. You sound a bit snappy." Richard's sister Thea's voice had a hint of laughter in it. "I remember you sounding like that when you were revising for exams and my best friend Alice who fancied you kept knocking on your door and asking daft questions about her homework."

Richard smiled in spite of himself. "You were both aggravating little madams from what I remember. Now, what can I do for you – you sound as if you've got your Mrs Organiser head on today."

"I've spoken to Ginny about everything," said Thea, "just so she can get the bedrooms ready. Julia is mad on pink so the bedroom that used to be mine will be perfect for her. Your new nanny, Maria, is staying with me at the moment. Julia loves her. She's Italian and her aunt in London is a friend of Ginny's."

"It will be strange having a child in the house," said Richard. Thoughts spiralled through his mind – memories of Helen and Julia together. Then of the dark days after Helen's untimely death and the constant questions from Julia he couldn't answer.

"Not just 'a child' Richard. Your daughter."

There was an awkward pause.

"Richard – it will be OK," said Thea. "You and Julia need to be together again. It's what Helen would have wanted."

Richard swallowed the lump in his throat. "I know Thea. You and Adam have been brilliant having her all this time. I know it's time I moved forward but it's so…"

"Well, Julia's really excited. All she keeps asking is 'how many sleeps is it until Daddy comes?' She did say she'd miss Josh, Ben and Charlie but I have a feeling she'll miss the dogs and the kitten more. She asked the other day if she could take Picasso, Renoir or Kitty with her."

"What did you tell her?"

"I said that maybe if she asked you nicely you might let her have a pet that she could look after her with a bit of help from you or Maria."

"Leave that with me," said Richard. "I've got a rabbit in my office at the moment that might fit the bill nicely."

"Have you been drinking?" asked Thea.

"Most certainly not," he said. "See you on Sunday."

Emily was surprised and relieved when Richard returned to the kitchen his face lit up with a smile.

She'd got Rufus out of his hutch and was cuddling him for comfort. He lay in her arms twitching his nose gently and she'd been telling him she was trying to do the best she could for him. All thoughts of tea and biscuits had been forgotten. Emily was upset because she'd made Richard angry. Now it seemed his bad temper was forgotten.

She put the rabbit back in his hutch and waited to see what he had to say.

"That was my sister on the phone. I think I've found a new home for Rufus."

"You have? Where?"

"Long and complicated story – but my daughter Julia is coming back to live with me and my sister thinks it would be a good idea to get her a pet. You have a rabbit that needs a new home. I think we've got a deal."

"Oh – thank you!" Emily was so excited she flung her arms round his neck and kissed him – and then drew back in horror at what she'd done. "Oh – sorry, I mean thank you from Rufus that he's got a lovely home to go to."

"I hope he's not going to kiss me," said Richard with a wry smile. "Come on, let's go and get him settled into his new home. I'll carry the hutch, you bring the bag with his stuff in it."

Emily got her handbag and the carrier bag with Rufus's food in it and followed Richard down the stairs.

Richard spread the picnic rug on the back seat again and placed the hutch on it. Rufus eyed him curiously as if to say 'where are we off to now?'

This time they headed out of town and along the lane that led to the church where Emily and Angie used to ride their bikes or go looking for wild flowers with Granddad Frank or Angie's aunt. Ada, for some reason, never wanted to walk this way. She always took them to the park at the other end of town.

As they drove along the lane bordered with wild roses and elderflower, Emily remembered how cross Ada had been when she and Angie came back and told her about the adventure they'd had playing 'truth or dare' and ended up picnicking in the little round marble folly opposite the church.

She'd gone pale like she did when she had a headache. "You girls shouldn't have done that," she said.

"We weren't doing any harm. We didn't leave any litter or disturb anything."

Emily remembered Granddad having a quiet word with Ada in the kitchen and how she'd put her arms round him and rested her head on his shoulder.

Later, she'd apologised to Emily for being cross with her. There was a hint of sadness in her voice and Emily wondered what had upset her.

Today as they drove past the small church with its square tower, Emily looked across the road to the folly on the other side of the stone wall. The gap in the wall that she and Angie had squeezed through had been repaired but the folly itself was only just visible due to overgrown brambles and ivy. Only the marble dome stuck out like a bald head with a fringe of green hair.

"My friend and I loved that little folly." Emily spoke without thinking.

Richard smiled. "You and half the youngsters in Marchwood I should think. You've no idea what my sister and I used to find in there."

"My grandmother told me off for going there. I expect she thought we'd get arrested or something."

"My mother loved it there too," said Richard. "She used to say it was haunted, but not in a nasty way, more like somebody watching over it. I just wish I had the money to renovate it. I like the idea of my daughter playing there like Thea and I used to."

Emily tried to imagine what it would be like to live somewhere like Oakwood House and have what looked like an endless playground outside the window. Her stomach rumbled loudly and she hoped Richard couldn't hear it.

He'd stopped the car outside some black wrought iron electronic gates that opened slowly when he pressed the dibber from the glove box. They turned in and drove along an avenue of beech trees where the sunlight filtered through the leaves and created patterns on the charcoal grey path.

Emily almost gasped when they emerged from the avenue of trees into full sunlight in front of a square white Georgian house with long sash windows and a carriage ring in front of it. There were five steps up to an imposing black front door framed by white pillars.

A plump woman with short dark hair, her clothes protected by a blue and white striped apron emerged from an archway with a basket full of tomatoes and lettuce and hurried towards the car.

Richard opened his window to talk to her.

"Mr Kingsley, I didn't expect you back yet."

"This is just a flying visit, Ginny. This is Miss Randall who has been working for me at my office. She has a rabbit that needs a new home – and at my sister's suggestion I'm having him as a pet for Julia."

"That's wonderful," said Ginny, "and it's lovely to meet you too Miss Randall. I'll be in the kitchen if either of you need anything."

She headed back the way she'd come with her basket of vegetables.

"Between Ginny and Julia that rabbit will end up like a barrel," said Richard. "Come on, I'll show you where I thought would be a good place for him. See what you think. We can leave him in the car with the windows open for a few minutes."

He got out of the car and came round and opened her door for her. Emily got out and followed him in the opposite direction to the one taken by Ginny, round the corner of the house and towards a lawn shaded by a cedar tree where there was a wooden summerhouse.

They were at the back of the house now. The summerhouse could be seen from a room that had French doors that opened onto a terrace.

Richard strode on ahead but Emily lagged behind. The combination of heat and hunger was doing strange things to her vision. She felt as if her head was full of cotton-wool, her legs felt wobbly and black specks danced in front of her eyes.

She remembered Richard turning back to say something to her and trying to reply through lips that suddenly felt numb. Her legs crumpled like an empty paper bag and for a few minutes everything went black.

Strong arms lifted her from the ground. She could feel the beat of his heart through his blue cotton shirt and smell his spicy aftershave. He carried her across to the terrace and in through the open French doors and laid her on one of the cream-coloured sofas.

Emily opened her eyes and found herself in the most beautiful room she'd ever seen. Richard was kneeling beside her. "You frightened me," he said. "What happened?"

"I get like that when I haven't eaten," said Emily feeling guilty for causing him worry. "I was going to have something when I came back to the office at lunch-time and then you'd found Rufus and I was too upset to have anything."

"You had breakfast, surely?"

Emily shook her head. "I had to get Rufus out of the way because the landlord was coming and my grandmother isn't supposed to have pets. We had to hide Nelson's food dishes and send him out in the garden."

"And who is Nelson?"

"He's my grandmother's one-eyed ginger tom. I rescued him when he was a kitten."

Emily glanced at Richard. He was laughing.

"Stay there. I'll go and sort Rufus out and see if Ginny can rustle us up a snack."

"Oh, I don't want to be a nuisance." Emily struggled to a sitting position.

"She likes looking after people."

While he was gone, Emily looked around the cream and pink room. Light flooded in through the long Georgian windows and the atmosphere was peaceful. There were beautiful patchwork cushions in pink and dark green on the cream sofas and a large polished table held a collection of photographs in silver frames.

Feeling a bit like an intruder, Emily studied the photographs. There were several of a beautiful woman and a little girl, both with blonde curls.

"That was Mr Kingsley's wife, Helen," said Ginny coming in with a tray that held mugs of hot chocolate and plates with thick slices of fruit cake. She moved two occasional tables closer to the sofa and placed a plate and a mug on each one.

"He must miss her dreadfully," said Emily.

"There was a time when I didn't think he'd ever get over it."

She didn't say any more. Richard had moved Rufus into the summerhouse and was now crossing the lawn towards the terrace and the French doors with long strides.

"He should be happy in there," he said as he came and sat on the sofa and picked up his mug of hot chocolate.

"Hot chocolate probably wasn't the best thing for a day like today but it's one of the best things I know for giving you an energy boost," said Ginny.

"It's wonderful, thank you," said Emily.

Ginny left and Emily and Richard ate their cake in companionable silence for a few moments.

"I love the cushions," said Emily. "The colours and shapes work really well together."

"My wife made them," said Richard. "The plan was to create a proper craft workshop here for her – but then…" His voice tailed off.

"Where did you meet her? She was very beautiful."

"We met at Art College. Originally, she wanted to do ceramics but then found textiles more fascinating."

Emily finished her hot chocolate and cake.

"You look better," said Richard. "When you're ready you can check that Rufus's new accommodation is to your satisfaction."

"He's a very lucky rabbit."

Emily got to her feet. As she did so, a photograph on the large table attracted her attention. It was a black and white photograph of a man in officer's uniform. He was sitting on a bench, a spaniel at his feet. There was something familiar about the picture but Emily couldn't remember why. She moved across the room and pointed to it.

"Who is this? I'm sure I've seen this photograph somewhere before, ages ago when I was a child."

"You can't have done."

"Who is it?"

"That's my Great Uncle Jack Kingsley. He survived the war, never settled when he got back here and then died suddenly on Valentine's Day 1946 with two tickets for a voyage to Canada in his pocket. We never found out who he was planning to go with."

Richard led the way through the entrance hall, noticing the way Emily gazed at everything as if studying it for an exam. He wondered what it was about her that made him feel so unsettled. He could smell her shampoo – coconut and lemon – and the memory of how she felt in his arms, the feel of her heartbeat through the thin fabric of her dress, teased his senses. He only just stopped himself from taking her hand in his as they went across the entrance hall, down the steps and back to his car.

A surprise greeted them when they got back to the office. The receptionist from the solicitors who occupied the ground floor came out to see Richard.

"You've got a visitor," she said shooting Richard a flirtatious glance from under her dark eyelashes. "I understand congratulations are in order. I must say you've kept that quiet."

"What do you mean?"

The receptionist swept him a look as if she was talking to a complete idiot. "Your fiancée has arrived. You weren't here. I let her in. She's upstairs waiting for you. With her luggage."

She went back into her office before Richard could say anything else.

Emily felt as if someone had thrown a bucket of cold water over her. The sensation of being in Richard's arms hadn't left her. She half-closed her eyes remembering his aftershave and the clean cotton smell of his shirt. She didn't understand what was going on. Richard had spoken of his wife so tenderly and appeared to miss her still. He'd said that the job in America had stopped him from going completely mad but he'd not said anything about meeting anyone out there or getting engaged.

Emily followed him up the stairs. The reception area was crowded with a stack of white and gold Louis Vuitton suitcases. A woman in a white linen dress and gold jewellery that looked so tacky it must be really expensive emerged from Richard's office.

Her blonde hair was immaculate and didn't look as if it would move in a strong wind, making Emily aware of her unruly dark curls.

She smiled at Richard, showing perfect teeth. "I couldn't wait any longer to see you, sweetie." She moved closer to him releasing a cloud of exotic perfume and put her arms out to him. "Don't I get a kiss?"

Emily beat a hasty retreat in the direction of her desk and pretended to sort the papers on it. The hot chocolate and fruit cake she'd had at Oakwood House made her feel queasy and her stomach churned.

Lacey and Richard emerged from his office and headed towards the kitchen.

"I guess this must be your secretary," drawled Lacey, shooting a barbed glance at Emily behind Richard's back.

"This is Emily," said Richard. "She's been helping me since my permanent secretary Monica went into hospital last week."

"I'm sure she's been very helpful," said Lacey glaring at Emily again.

Richard headed out to the kitchen and switched the kettle on. Lacey followed and looked through the cupboards. "I don't see any organic green tea," she said. "And what are these cookies doing here? I didn't think you ate trash like that, Ritchie."

Emily noticed Richard wince at the shortening of his name. He'd told her his sister's full name was

Dorothea, shortened to Thea, whereas he'd always refused to answer to anything but Richard. Until now, obviously.

Lacey opened the fridge, crouching down on her high heels as she examined the contents. "Gee – what's all this full fat milk and yogurt? I don't want you having a heart attack Ritchie." She swept a honeyed look at him.

"That's mine," said Emily, picking up the milk and yogurt before they followed the biscuits into the rubbish bin. She shot a look at Richard. He didn't say anything and his eyes appeared to be focused somewhere outside the window.

Emily fetched her time-sheet. "Can you sign this please, Mr Kingsley." She noticed how he blinked at the formality in her voice but he scribbled his signature at the bottom of the document. She put it in her bag, gabbled a hasty goodbye and left the building.

It was only when Emily got outside the building, she realised how wobbly her legs felt. She felt confused. A very short time ago she just wanted to be with Richard. She'd thought after the way James had let her down that she'd never trust another man but when she'd fainted and Richard had carried her indoors it had felt right being in his arms.

Lacey was here and everything had changed.

## CHAPTER FIVE

Emily was in such a state she'd gone several hundred yards along the road before she remembered the pram. She hurried back for it knowing Ada wouldn't be happy if she returned home without it. As she did so, Richard's car swept out of the car park. Lacey was sitting beside him in the passenger seat. They didn't notice her.

She felt self-conscious pushing an empty pram along the High Street, particularly when people stopped her to look in it and then gave her weird looks when they saw it was empty. Early that morning when she took Rufus to the office there were very few people about.

She headed to the Agency to drop her time sheet in. She parked the pram outside, remembering to put the brake on.

Glenda looked up from her desk when Emily walked in and then peered outside at the pram. "Good heavens, someone's left a baby outside."

"No they haven't," said Emily. "It's a long story but the pram belongs to my grandmother and I used it to take a rabbit to work with me this morning."

A smile broke out across Glenda's face. "Not the rabbit that's been on You Tube?"

"I hope not," said Emily, imagining what Richard's reaction would be if he knew Rufus was becoming a star. She handed over her time sheet. It would seem a long time until she got paid next Friday.

"How was the job?" asked Glenda. "I've heard he's a lovely man."

"Fine," said Emily. "And yes, he is." The memory of being in his arms brought a blush to her cheeks.

It had been fine until Lacey arrived. While they'd had their hot chocolate and cake, Richard had talked about the projects he'd be working on the following week. He'd confided in her about how worried he was as to whether Julia would settle with the new nanny and whether she'd be happy back at Oakwood House.

"Of course she will," Emily had said. "She'll have you – and Rufus."

She'd been rewarded with a smile that lit up his sea-green eyes.

He'd asked her if she was close to her own father. Emily had mentioned her parents' divorce when she was in her teens but that she still had a special relationship with her Dad even if she didn't see him very often.

He'd nodded in sympathy and they'd spent a few moments in companionable silence.

"Here's your time sheet for next week. As far as I know the regular secretary Monica will be out of action for at least six weeks. Keep up the good work," said Glenda.

Emily folded the time sheet and put it in her bag. As she got to her feet and headed towards the door, the phone rang. Glenda picked it up.

Emily mouthed 'goodbye' to her but Glenda motioned her to stay where she was.

The call didn't take long. The message was delivered briefly and precisely.

"That was a call from Richard Kingsley's office. Apparently you're not wanted next week after all. His fiancée has just arrived from America and will take care of everything."

"So what do I do?" Emily felt numb. "Is there anything else you can offer me?"

"Not until next week unfortunately – unless anything unexpected happens. Your money for this week will be paid into your bank account next Friday. I'll let you know as soon as there's a suitable vacancy."

Emily left the Agency, feeling foolish as she pushed the empty pram down the road. She felt frustrated that her attempt to build up some money had been blocked and hurt that Richard couldn't tell her to her face that she wasn't wanted any more.

She was on her way to the Library to look up any suitable vacancies online when a white van screeched to a halt next to her. Emily stopped, expecting to see a driver in need of directions. Instead, Angie got out and headed towards her looking excited.

"Emily, you didn't say anything about having a baby."

"I haven't," said Emily giving her a playful shove. "This is Gran's old pram, remember? The one we used to take turns to push our dolls in, plus any shopping she wanted."

"I'm surprised it's still going. What are you doing with it?"

"Long story," said Emily.

"I'm all ears. Why don't we put the pram in the back of the van and then I can give you a guided tour of my café and you can tell me what you're doing back in Marchwood."

When they got to the café they rang Angie's aunt who still lived next door to Ada and asked her to tell her that Emily would be home later than expected.

The café was like a giant log cabin that smelled of fresh paint inside and out. The outside was painted marshmallow pink and the walls inside were dazzling white. The main entrance to it was opposite the children's playground – a place where Emily and Angie had spent lots of time when they were children. A door at the far end led to a quiet terrace bordered with trellises hung with sweet peas and morning glories that were a riot of colour and scent.

It was here that they sat nursing mugs of tea while Emily told Angie about her failed romance and the collapse of her artistic dreams.

"I discovered a long time ago that all men are rats," said Angie stirring in extra sugar. "I haven't found one yet who hasn't let me down. I thought the last one – Raoul from Barcelona – was going to be different. He looked fabulous and he was going to paint me some pictures for the café walls. Then I caught him red-handed trying to steal the paint and canvases as well as money from the till. When I challenged him about it he went all '*no speak Engleesh*' on me." She drained her cup. "So that's it. No more men for me."

"They're not all like that," said Emily thinking of Richard and how much he'd clearly loved his wife – and how good it had felt being in his arms. She paused. She'd thought he liked working with her but then he'd let her down by saying he didn't want her to work for him anymore.

Angie was looking at her with an amused glint in her blue eyes. "Something's happened. Tell me more. You're not leaving here until you do…"

Emily told her about her fainting fit at Oakwood House that afternoon.

"Nothing new there then," said Angie. "Do you remember that talent show we did at school for an animal rescue centre and you wouldn't stop for a break and ended up going wobbly when you came off the stage and that lad from the sixth form carried you into the classroom. I think he fancied his chances."

"Yes I do remember," said Emily with a shudder. "He had chronic acne and bad breath."

"It wasn't like that today then?" said Angie. They'd progressed from tea to glasses of wine.

"Definitely not," said Emily. "It felt…" She took a sip of wine and tried to cool her flaming cheeks. "Anyway, regardless of how I feel, he's obviously got his hands full with Miss America. It's just weird that he didn't say anything about her."

"How do you know it wasn't her that made the call to the Agency?"

"Why would she do that?"

Angie shrugged. "It depends how determined she is to see off any opposition. Pretty much so I'd say if she's travelled all that way."

Angie drove Emily and the pram back to Ada's house.

"You could come and do some work for me," she said as she pulled up outside.

"That's very kind of you," said Emily her eyes filling with unexpected tears, "but I don't expect charity."

"It wouldn't be," said Angie. "I'm one person short because Raoul has done a disappearing act. I've hired a new girl but she can't start till next week. Even when she does it would be wonderful if you could slosh some paint on those canvases and liven the walls up a bit."

"Do you mean 'create some paintings'?" asked Emily with a wicked grin.

"Something like that."

"Provided you keep me supplied with tea and some of those naughty-looking flapjacks then you're on."

Emily lay in bed that night, her mind a curious mixture of emotions. The full moon shone through the curtains like a searchlight beam as her mind raked over the events of the day.

It was when she thought of the drawing room at Oakwood House and the silver-framed photographs on the polished wooden table that she remembered where she'd seen the one of Jack Kingsley before.

That same picture was in a newspaper cutting she'd once found in a wooden box in Ada's dressing table when she was playing a dressing up game when she was a child. She'd been too young to read the article but she remembered asking Ada who the man in the soldier's uniform was.

"That's for me to know and you to find out when you're older," had been Ada's enigmatic response. The expression on her face told Emily that was the only answer she was going to get.

The next time she'd been allowed to play in Ada's dressing table, the photograph was gone.

# CHAPTER SIX

Thea Stanton was fast running out of patience. She'd got up early that Sunday morning to make sure the day went as smoothly as possible. She knew how insecure her brother Richard felt about living with his daughter again. Thea's heart ached when she thought of how like her mother Helen little Julia was and how difficult this must be for him.

Richard knew Thea couldn't have Julia on a permanent basis. The arrangement had only ever been temporary. It needed to end now because Thea's husband Mark had been offered a work placement in New Zealand for six months.

As usual when she was under stress, Thea relied on good planning to get her through the day. Her intended early start had been impeded by five year old Julia coming into her room at six thirty dressed in her cousin's black and white football socks pulled up to her thighs and a fairy costume complete with glittery pink wings and starry wand.

"Kitty's just been sick," she lisped. She didn't like the cornflakes I gave her."

Thea sighed and got out of bed, leaving her husband Adam to snore, something Julia found funny and Thea (having put up with it for nearly twelve years) found intensely irritating.

"Uncle Adam sounds like a walrus," she said.

"Where's Maria?" asked Thea. "Why isn't she looking after you?"

"She said: "*Lulia eet ees too early. I sleep. You sleep.*" I don't want to sleep any more. I want to wait for Daddy."

"He'll be here soon. We've got lots to do before then," said Thea pulling on her red dressing gown and matching slippers and heading downstairs to the kitchen.

Julia followed her and Thea felt a touch of sadness. She'd longed for a daughter with each of her pregnancies and it had been nice having dolls and teddies around the house instead of the endless tide of footballs and boisterous games.

Thea cleared up after Kitty who was now sitting by the Aga, green eyes focused on the shelf where her food was kept, tortoiseshell tail swishing. Picasso and Dali, the two golden Labradors thumped their tails enthusiastically.

"Don't think you're getting a walk yet," said Thea. She hoped Adam and the boys might take them out before Richard arrived.

Thea didn't know why she felt uneasy about today – it was only Sunday lunch with her brother. She switched on the kettle, spooned instant coffee into a mug, poured juice for Julia and put four slices of raisin bread into the toaster. As she sipped her coffee she went through her list again. Melon to start with sprinkled with ginger, then roast chicken, stuffing, boiled potatoes, roast potatoes, parsnips, cauliflower cheese, carrots, peas and gravy. Apple crumble and clotted cream for pudding.

She went into the dining room that overlooked the front garden. The house was a rambling Victorian former vicarage and the gardens, front and back, were a riot of cottage garden plants. Roses and honeysuckle rampaged over trellises and the borders were crammed with hollyhocks, delphiniums and columbines. Bees droned lazily amongst lavender and rosemary and the children had fun making dens in the shrubbery.

Thea looked at the dining table and decided against laying it formally with a white cloth and the best cutlery. It only made more things to nag the children for – and she was sure Richard would be happier with something more relaxed. She spread the faded blue patchwork tablecloth Helen had made for her over the table and set it picnic-style with an unmatched assortment of side plates. Julia helped, insisting on her favourite one with the peacock on it.

Adam emerged eventually, yawning and stretching, hair on end, followed by the three boys. They had their breakfast sitting at the kitchen table, the dogs fussing around them. Thea was busy making apple crumble, her hands covered in flour. The chicken was bubbling and spitting in the oven and the roast potatoes and parsnips, golden with oil and fragrant with rosemary, were waiting to go in.

Julia was sitting at the far end of the kitchen table, still wearing her fairy outfit, busy drawing a picture that involved a lot of green and purple glitter and silver stars.

Thea knew from some training she'd done at Playgroup that you weren't supposed to ask a child what a picture was meant to be.

"Tell me about your picture," she asked when Julia announced she'd finished and could she please have a drink.

"It's a picture of Mummy in the ball gown she wore when she went to Heaven. Then that's her dancing among the stars. Will Daddy bring her back with him today?"

The question brought a lump to Thea's throat. "No darling, Mummy's gone to Heaven to be an angel."

Thankfully at that moment, the beep of her mobile showed a text message had arrived. It was from Richard: *'See you at 12. Am bringing Lacey with me. Hope that is OK.'*

Thea's mind span backwards. She knew Richard had said on the phone that he'd got a rabbit for Julia. Maybe he was bringing it with him. It seemed an odd thing to do because Julia and Maria had lots of luggage – but that was typical of Richard not to think about things like that.

"Was that Daddy?" asked Julia.

"Yes," said Thea, "and he's bringing someone special to meet you."

"Is it a doggy or a pussycat?" Julia's face sparkled with excitement.

"We'll have to wait and see won't we? Now where's Maria? It's time she had her breakfast or she won't want any lunch."

Adam had gone out, taking the boys and the dogs with him. Smells of roasting chicken and fragrant herbs drifted through the house. Thea began to relax. She'd been silly to feel uneasy. Everything was under control.

Maria emerged, dressed in a pink tracksuit, her dark hair bundled into a ponytail. She refused an offer of breakfast but did accept a mug of strong coffee. "At home we no eat breakfast," she said. "In Italia, we go to café later and have coffee and biscotti."

"I hope you'll make sure Julia has a proper breakfast," said Thea, aware she was sounding a bit prim and proper.

"Of course," said Maria.

Adam, the boys and the dogs had returned, causing chaos. Maria picked up her mug of coffee and moved towards the playroom where the three boys were putting their railway track together amid a lot of good-tempered banter.

The dogs headed for their water bowls, slobbering eagerly and getting more on the floor than into themselves.

Adam came up behind Thea, put his arms round her and nuzzled her neck. "Everything alright? There's something about you in an apron that really drives me wild."

Thea flicked a tea towel at him and carried on stirring the bread sauce, hoping Richard wasn't going to be too much later. She'd told him twelve thirty for one and it was already ten to one. It was unlike him to be late."

"Sort some wine for us and some drinks for the kids will you?" she asked Adam.

The eldest boy, Josh, rushed in to announce that Uncle Richard had just arrived and that he'd brought a lady with him. "She looks like the Snow Queen," he said.

Thea's response was a flash of irritation with her brother. It wasn't like him to be so insensitive. Today was meant to be a special time for him and Julia. She'd gone to so much trouble to plan a day that they'd all remember and now it seemed that they would do so but for the wrong reasons.

Her heart sank as she looked at the dining table. What had looked casual and inviting a few moments ago, more like an indoor picnic, now just looked messy. Thea hurried to lay an extra place and then went to greet her brother and his mystery guest.

Out in the hallway Richard and the woman were being greeted by an overwhelming mixture of children and dogs. Thea smiled in spite of feelings of tension that were making her head ache. Josh's description was exactly right. This woman did look like the Snow Queen. White was the worst possible colour to wear to a house full of children and dogs – particularly as Julia had launched herself at Richard's legs, eager to show him her picture. In doing so, she'd scattered pink and green glitter over immaculate Capri pants.

"Let them get in the door," Thea urged, noticing how the woman's mouth was set in a disapproving line. "Go and sit up at the table kids, dinner is nearly ready."

"Lacey, Richard, come and take the weight off your feet," said Adam after Richard had made the introductions, explaining they were late because Lacey couldn't decide what to wear.

"A girl likes to look her best," drawled Lacey, flicking a disapproving glance over Thea's jeans and sweatshirt.

"Wine, beer or cider?" asked Adam as he took Lacey's jacket.

"Just organic mineral water for me," said Lacey taking her place at the table as far away as possible from children and dogs.

"We only have tap water or tonic water," said Adam.

"I guess it will have to be tap," said Lacey looking as if he'd suggested she drink engine oil.

Thea and Maria carried dishes of food in from the kitchen. Thea had carved the chicken and the slices of it edged with golden skin looked succulent and delicious. They could only just fit everything on the table.

"It looks great," said Richard.

He looked tired, thought Thea, and ill at ease for all that he'd joined in some of the rough and tumble with the boys and had made a fuss of the dogs. She'd so hoped things would go well today and that Julia would adapt easily to her new life back at Oakwood House.

Conversation around the table had risen to a pitch of excitement while the plates were being carried in. Julia insisted on sitting next to Richard although this placed her between him and Lacey. Thea could see from the expression on the American girl's face that this wasn't going down well – and neither was the food.

"Oh gee, didn't Ritchie say? I only eat grilled fish and steamed vegetables." She swept a disapproving glance over the food Thea had prepared so carefully. "When I first met Ritchie I was horrified at the amount of junk food he was eating."

"You can't beat a good English roast dinner," said Richard a little too heartily in an attempt to defray the tense atmosphere. He helped himself from the dish of chicken Adam offered him and put some on Julia's plate.

"Can I get you anything else, Lacey?" asked Thea in clipped tones.

"No, thank you." She flashed perfect white teeth. "I'll make do with some boiled potatoes and carrots."

"Daddy, why didn't you tell us Lacey was a lady?" asked Julia when her plate was empty. "Auntie Thea said you were bringing a dog."

Adam bit back a yelp of laughter. "Seconds anyone?" he asked, heading towards the kitchen.

When he came back a few minutes later he was carrying a dish that contained the remains of the chicken, stuffing and roast potatoes. There was a glint in his dark eyes that Thea noticed and felt heartened by.

"So how's it going with sorting out your father's affairs?" Adam asked Richard.

Richard pulled a face. "Let's just say we could do with finding Great Uncle Jack's lost treasure," he said.

Thea smiled. "We spent hours searching various nooks and crannies for it, didn't we? And in all likelihood it was probably just one of Dad's stories"

"I suppose we'll never know now," said Richard.

"Great Uncle Jack," he said to Lacey, "is one of the family mysteries. He survived the Second World War with barely a scratch and then died on Valentine's Day 1946 from a heart attack in his bedroom. He had two tickets for a one way voyage to Canada in his pocket."

"Who was he going with?" asked Lacey.

"We have no idea."

The dinner plates were cleared and Thea brought in the apple crumble and cream. "There's cheese and biscuits if anyone's still hungry after that," she said, ignoring Lacey's look of disapproval.

"The dessert looks delicious but I'll just have a few grapes if that's OK," she said. "I have to think of my figure." She flashed a flirtatious look at Richard which Thea noticed he didn't return.

Richard knew as soon as he'd arrived here that it had been a mistake to bring Lacey. She didn't fit in here. Two images fought for space inside his head – Lacey pecking at the green grapes like a sparrow and the other of Emily tucking into Ginny's fruit cake as if food was her greatest passion in life, her face lit up with happiness. He had a feeling if Emily was here now she'd be enjoying the party.

*"What's the matter with you?"* he said to himself. *"It's Lacey who pulled you back from the brink after Helen died. She's only showing she cares now."*

So why did he feel panicky again when he looked at Lacey sitting beside him. It reminded him of the terrible days after Helen had died – a feeling as if he was a character in a horror film trying to escape from a room that was growing steadily smaller.

Lacey lost no time in calling her friend Gloria in New York as soon as they got back to Oakwood House. She'd felt out of place all day, had realised she should have stayed out of the picture until Richard came back, but her childhood fear of being left out had made her insist on going with him.

She'd felt irritated to be banished to the back seat with the hired help for the journey home while Richard's obnoxious brat sat in the front passenger seat. What was worse was having to listen to the child chattering all the way home. Lacey had forgotten her headphones in the rush to leave the house.

"I felt sure Ritchie would be sending her away to school," she complained to Gloria.

"I don't understand why you went after him in such a hurry," said Gloria, "especially if you don't like being in the country, you hate the food and you don't want to live with his daughter."

"My father likes him. He's always wanted me to marry an Englishman – and until I'm married he won't let me have the money my grandfather left me. If I didn't know better I'd say he was up to something. He'd got that 'I'm expanding my business empire' glint in his eye the last time I saw him."

"So what does Richard say about it all?"

"Nothing yet – but I don't think he'll have any choice but to marry me. From what I heard he wants to keep his house really badly – and he's in poor shape financially."

"So you haven't told him anything yet?"

"No – it's never the right time."

"And you think he'll agree to this?"

"I'll have him eating out of my hand."

Julia had enjoyed the journey home, sat in the front seat of the car with her Daddy. The last few moments before they left Auntie Thea's were a bit strange. There had been a whispered discussion between Auntie Thea and her Daddy that sounded like wasps buzzing in a jar.

Then Auntie Thea had given her a big kiss and a cuddle and said they'd all see her again very soon. Julia wondered why she looked like she'd been crying when she said it.

Julia thought Lacey was a silly name. It was funny that she went to the wrong side of the car as if she was going to drive and not Daddy. Julia had got in the front passenger seat and Daddy strapped her in. Maria was already sitting in the back.

"Is Lacey going home with them or is she going back to America?" Josh had asked, his clear voice carrying down the drive.

Uncle Adam had looked like he was choking again which was strange because he wasn't eating anything.

Lacey had got in the back next to Maria. Daddy started the car and they'd driven off with a lot of waving and shouting from Auntie Thea and the cousins.

At the house, they'd been greeted by a smiling Ginny who had offered them tea and orange juice. She'd also made some butterfly cakes with pink icing.

"A little bird told me it's a little girl called Julia's favourite colour," she'd said.

"What about her teeth?" Lacey said, "Not to mention all the fat and sugar."

"She can clean them at bed time," said Ginny in a voice that brooked no argument. "And you can't have a welcome home party without cake."

Ginny disappeared back to the kitchen saying that supper would be at eight.

Julia had seen her bedroom and she liked the shell-pink walls and matching bed cover and curtains. Daddy had taken her to meet Rufus and had shown her the instructions a lady called Emily had written out for her. Julia liked the little pictures she'd done, particularly the one of Rufus eating a carrot.

Maria had also liked her room which she said reminded her of Italian sunflowers.

Julia knew she'd lived here before, when she was tiny. There were photos in the sitting room of her playing with Mummy in the garden and pushing her tiny doll's pram. The memories Julia had were just isolated images – the front steps, the black and white pattern of the entrance hall floor and the view of the cedar tree from the sitting room. She could remember the feel of her mother's hair against her cheek when she kissed her goodnight and the perfume she always wore that came from a purple bottle on her dressing table.

As she went along blue carpeted upstairs corridor towards the curved staircase, she wished her cousins were here to explore with her. They could have great fun playing hide and seek. However, when she reached the partly-open door to Lacey's room she was glad they weren't here.

Lacey was talking to someone on the phone. Her voice was low, as if she was afraid of being overheard. At first it didn't sound very interesting but then Julia heard her name mentioned and stopped. She held her breath in an effort not to make a noise, even though she had a prickly feeling behind her eyes and nose as if she was going to cry.

"There's no way I want to play step-mother." Lacey was saying. "If Ritchie accepts my offer of marriage then I'm going to suggest he sends Julia away to school. I don't see it working otherwise with her coming between us all the time."

There was a pause while Lacey listened to what the person on the other end of the phone had to say. Julia fidgeted from one foot to the other, anxious not to make any noise.

"Yes – sure my Pa will be happy if I marry Ritchie. He always wanted me to marry an Englishman. The way I look at it, we'd both be winners. Ritchie would get to keep his house and I'd get to inherit the money and be able to do whatever I want – which as you and I know is a very cute guy in New York called Luca."

There was the sound of Lacey opening and shutting drawers and a few bursts of laughter.

Julia moved away, her heart feeling as if it was bouncing like Auntie Thea's washing machine with an uneven load. She didn't understand any of it. Something was wrong like the time they told her one of the guinea pigs was 'a little bit poorly' and the next time she went to look for him he wasn't there anymore.

This had the same feel of not being told the truth and Julia didn't like it. If Daddy was going to forget about Mummy and marry someone else he should have told her.

The thought occurred to her that maybe he couldn't because Lacey was always around and he wanted to talk to her on her own. Julia decided she'd ask him about it at breakfast time if she could get him on his own without *her* being there. Julia swallowed hard. It felt as if there was a lump in her throat. She had a feeling she might not like the answer he'd give her.

Julia remembered a story Auntie Thea had read them one night about some children who ran away from home because they didn't want to be sent away to school. She decided that's what she would do if her Daddy married Lacey.

# CHAPTER SEVEN

Emily was so busy on Saturday helping Angie at the café that she didn't have time to brood about the way her job working for Richard Kingsley had come to an end.

On Friday evening Ada had told Emily she was going on a coach trip to Weston-Super-Mare with the Darby & Joan Club the following day.

"I wasn't going," she said, "but then when Molly next door came round and said you and Angie were having fun together at the café I decided I would." She looked at Emily. "You will be alright won't you? I'll be leaving early. Eight o'clock at the Post Office, Molly says."

Emily assured her that she'd be fine helping Angie.

"As if you don't work hard enough," said Ada. "That's one thing you and I have in common, Emily. We're both Saturday's children. We work hard for our living."

Emily smiled. She remembered Ada reciting the rhyme that began "Monday's child is fair of face..." when she'd stayed here as a child.

"You will feed Nelson won't you before you go out? He doesn't like me going out and he gets really difficult and won't eat his breakfast. You might have more success than me."

"Don't worry, he'll be fine," said Emily. "He doesn't look in any danger of starvation."

She and Ada were both up early for a breakfast of tea and toast. Then Ada left the house wearing black trousers and her new purple jumper and carrying enough food in her quilted holdall to feed the entire coach.

"Anyone would think you had a secret assignation. You're wearing your best perfume," said Emily giving her grandmother a hug.

"I couldn't be bothered with a man at my age," said Ada with a sad smile.

She looked as if she was going to say something else, but at that moment Molly knocked on the door, worried they were going to be late and the two of them went off together through the archway of hollyhocks and out of the front gate.

After Ada had gone, Emily washed up the breakfast things and put some food down for Nelson. He came strutting in from the back garden, looking as if he owned the place and proceeded to sniff around the entire house as if to make sure Rufus had truly gone.

"Rufus won't be back, Nelson," said Emily. "He's gone to live at Richard's house."

Memories of the previous day flooded back, the sensation of being in Richard's arms, the texture of his shirt next to her skin and the salty smell of his sweat. She was sure she hadn't mistaken the feeling of closeness that had developed between them – something that felt natural and right – quickly extinguished by the unexpected arrival of Lacey.

Nelson purred loudly and rubbed himself around her legs as if to reassure Emily he was there and still loved her. She picked him up and gave him a hug and then set him back down by his food bowl. He ate a few mouthfuls as if doing it to please her and then sat and stared up at her with his piercing yellow eye.

Emily's mobile bleeped. Angie had sent her a text. *"R u still coming 2 the café 2day?"*

*"Yes – won't be long,"* she sent back.

She gave herself a talking to. Last night she and Angie had drunk a toast to ‘new beginnings.’ “Every day is a fresh start,” said one of the inspirational notices on the café wall. Emily blew a kiss to Nelson, picked up her bag and hurried out of the door.

She felt differently when she got to the café and saw the early morning buzz of customers – joggers and cyclists stopping for a restorative mug of tea and some cinnamon toast, families with children making an early visit to the swings and calling in for glasses of orange juice.

Angie looked as if she was in her element, chatting and smiling as she poured tea and helped children choose the biggest slice of cake.

Emily joined in and helped as best she could, clearing tables and doing the washing up. When they had a lull, Angie directed her towards the far end of the café where she’d set up a couple of large tables in a screened off area that she’d said she hoped to develop for mysteriously named ‘other activities.’

When Emily saw the paint, brushes and canvases that Angie had placed there for her, she felt light-headed with anxiety remembering how her previous attempt to be an artist had ended up.

“What did we say last night, Emily?” asked Angie. “You are an artist. Look at all the work you completed and sold before you even met James. Anyway, what have you got to lose? Just think how much of a favour you’d be doing me – and it’s better than washing up isn’t it?”

Emily hesitated.

“Look,” said Angie, “I’d slosh some paint on the canvases myself if I had a spare minute between customers. It can’t be that difficult.”

Emily laughed at this. "From what you said about your school days, you were as good in art lessons as I was at cookery. My Gran and your Auntie used to talk about putting us both in a sack and shaking us so that it mixed up our abilities a bit more."

Angie was laughing now. "Mug of tea and a chocolate brownie every hour as well as the going rate of pay? That's my best offer. You don't have to produce masterpieces. I just want something to liven up the walls."

"OK." Emily held her hands up in surrender. "I'll tell myself I'm not really painting, I'm livening up the walls."

She headed towards the far end of the café, pushed two large tables together, spread plastic sheets on them and the floor to protect them and looked at the selection of brushes and paints. She sat and thought for a while, looking out at the oak and horse chestnut trees bordering the play area.

Emily noticed a small boy in a red t-shirt crouching by one of the trees to post what looked like a secret wish in the roots of a giant oak. The idea came to her that she could paint a series of mystical trees for the café. It was different from anything she'd done before but it might be just what she needed to move on from the dark place she was in at the moment.

She prepared the first canvas and selected the colours she would use – silver, forest green and lilac. When Angie brought her first mug of tea, she ran the idea past her.

"Great idea – you go, girl!" was Angie's enthusiastic response before she headed back to the counter to serve a noisy group of cyclists.

Before long, Emily had attracted an enthusiastic audience, all eager to see 'the artist lady' at work. She was enjoying experimenting with the acrylic paint that Angie had supplied and the first painting of a mystical-looking tree surprised and delighted her because it was different from anything she'd done before.

She'd included a tiny figure at the base of the tree in memory of the little boy who had given her the idea.

"Looks like you could write a fairy-tale from that," said a solidly-built man with spiky brown hair sitting at a table near the window.

Emily, who had moved away from the painting to see if there was anything else she needed to add, smiled at him. He had an expensive-looking camera on the table beside him and was scribbling in an ink-stained notebook.

Angie came across with the Earl Grey tea and coffee and walnut cake the man had ordered.

"I shouldn't really be eating this," he said, indicating a waist-line that could best be described as 'cuddly.' "Food journalist is the wrong job for someone like me who can't resist delicious looking cakes."

"Food journalist?" said Angie, her face lighting up. "Tell me more."

"I'm touring the area, trying different places, getting some ideas for an article. Looks like you've got an interesting set-up here with the art as well as great food." He had to raise his voice, the café had been invaded by a family with a squalling toddler. "Do you do classes here?" he asked Emily.

Emily was just about to say she was only following Angie's instructions to create something to brighten the walls, when her friend shot her a warning glance.

"Yes – she will be," said Angie, ignoring Emily's panic-stricken look. "For all age groups."

Earlier a harassed looking mother had said how great it would be if somewhere like this did something to occupy her children while she drank a cup of coffee without having to answer a million and one questions. Angie hadn't said much then, but Emily had noticed the thoughtful look on her friend's face.

The man, who introduced himself as Nick Harvey, jotted down some details about them in his notebook and took some photos of the café, of Angie and Emily posing by the counter and of Emily's painting.

"I'll be in touch when I've got some news about the article," he said as he finished his tea and left.

"And that's probably the last we'll hear from him," said Angie under her breath. Emily didn't say anything. She didn't expect anything positive to come from the encounter either. Events from the past had left her feeling raw and fragile – like a crab without its shell. She'd loved James and trusted him and look where that had got her. Then in no time at all, she'd started having feelings for Richard and he'd also shown himself to be unreliable. No – it would be a long time before she trusted a man again.

"When did you say the art workshops for children were starting?" asked a woman with short dark hair who'd watched the photo shoot with interest.

"On Wednesday morning," said Angie. "Ten thirty." She gathered together a tray-full of dirty crockery, ignoring Emily's panic-stricken look, and headed towards the kitchen.

"What did you say that for?" asked Emily following her to the kitchen and leaning against the door so that Angie couldn't get out until she'd answered her question. "I thought I was helping you run the café, not running a crèche. I've not worked with children before – I might not be any good at it. And besides, don't you have to be officially checked by someone?"

"They'll have their parents or grandparents with them so I don't think it applies," said Angie. "Anyway, look how good you are with cute furry animals. Children aren't that different, or so I'm told! And if it gets more people into the café it's got to be worth trying." Angie stared imploringly at Emily.

"Oh, alright then!" said Emily. "I'll give it a try – although I'll probably live to regret it."

"Yes!" Angie punched the air in triumph as she left the café kitchen and head out to collect more washing up. "I knew you'd see it my way."

Sunday was another hectic day in the café. Emily worked on a new canvas, choosing a combination of lemon, caramel and gold paint and creating another of her fairy-tale trees. She viewed the growing list of names on the 'Paint a Story' workshop list with feelings of anxiety that made even Angie's cakes less tempting than usual.

Angie seemed to be on the phone as much as she was serving behind the counter. A lady who had seen yesterday's painting had called to ask if Angie would be interested in holding some art and craft exhibitions. A local group was interested in attending some cookery demonstrations.

After closing time, they sat with mugs of tea and slices of apple cake listing as many ideas as they could that would persuade people to visit the café.

"Talks and demonstrations," said Angie, "or set up a book group."

"Vintage tea parties."

"Health and fitness," said Angie.

"You'd have to take cakes and ice cream off the menu," said Emily. "They'd rather defeat the object."

They both collapsed in giggles.

Angie's phone rang again. She answered it, a smile like melted honey spreading across her face.

"It's Nick," she mouthed.

Emily looked confused until the penny dropped that it was the journalist who'd taken their photos the day before. From the drift of the conversation he was talking about more than the article.

"His editor loved his idea," she said when the call finished, "and he wants to take me out for a drink to celebrate. The article will be in 'The Guardian' later this week.

"I'd want to see the article first before I committed to anything," said Emily. "Just to make sure he's for real."

Angie laughed off Emily's downbeat response.

"I was going to say, before Nick rang, we could have speed dating evenings here. You could invite your Richard Kingsley."

"He's not my Richard Kingsley," said Emily, feeling an ache in her heart. "I've told you, he's spoken for."

## CHAPTER EIGHT

Richard was relieved that Julia and her nanny Maria appeared to be settling happily at Oakwood House. It was love at first sight between Julia and Rufus and Richard was touched to hear his daughter talking to the rabbit as if he was her new best friend.

On Monday evening, Julia was full of excitement. Richard was home from work early after a difficult day. He was relieved that Lacey had gone to her room pleading a headache, although minutes later he was sure he could hear her on the phone.

Richard, hearing excited giggles, headed towards the source of the noise and was in time to see Julia in her bath, playing happily with the bubbles and with a smiling Maria telling her the parts of the body in Italian.

"Daddy!" shrieked Julia stretching out her soapy arms and getting a torrent of water on the floor which Maria tried valiantly to mop up with a towel.

Richard submitted to a damp embrace, feeling touched that she was so happy to see him.

"Have you had a good day?" he asked them both.

They both nodded enthusiastically.

"We went of a bus ride to look at my new school. Then we went to the swings and a nasty boy tried to push me off the roundabout."

Richard stifled a grin, wishing that a nasty boy on the roundabout had been the worst thing that had happened to him that day.

"The best thing," said Julia, "was the pink café with the lady in the butterfly t-shirt. We drew pictures together."

"Don't you usually eat cakes in a café?" asked Richard.

Maria smiled.

"We did that as well," said Julia, "but the pictures were the best thing."

Richard waited until Julia was out of the bath, dried and in her pyjamas ready for bed. Ginny had made tea for her earlier. The adults would eat later in the evening.

Richard thought he'd get away with kissing Julia goodnight, but she put her arms round his neck, reminding him poignantly of Helen, and asked if he'd read her a story.

He sat on her bed and read her 'Cinderella', aware that his heart wasn't really in it.

"Daddy, you missed a page," said Julia. "The story doesn't go like that. She gets a visit from the fairy godmother before she gets to go to the ball."

Somehow, Richard got through the story, kissed Julia goodnight and then escaped for a few moments to his room where he opened the window and leaned out, relishing the feel of the warm breeze ruffling his hair carrying the scent of newly mown grass.

He closed his eyes, allowing the breeze to carry away some of the tension of the day. He'd gone into work with Lacey in tow, eager to make things up with Emily. He was aware they'd parted on slightly strange terms on Friday and he didn't know what to say when he did see her.

In the finish, his carefully rehearsed words weren't needed because she didn't turn up. He had no idea why and scribbled a note to himself to check with the agency when he had a spare moment.

Lacey had expressed surprise that Emily wasn't there.

"Maybe she needed to visit the dentist," she said. "Let me help you for now."

Richard had been unsettled by Lacey's unexpected arrival on Friday but didn't feel he could ask too bluntly why she'd travelled to England without letting him know she was doing so. He knew he owed her a lot - his current well-being and his sanity – and so was reluctant to upset her. When he'd arrived in America, newly bereaved and in a complete mess, it had been Lacey who had taken him under her wing, organised his work schedule and given structure to his days.

He'd not been able to say a proper goodbye to her when he got the phone call from his financial advisor because she was on holiday with a friend. He'd meant to write and say how grateful he'd been for her company and her help but somehow this hadn't happened.

Then as soon as he got back, he'd been caught up in the financial mess caused by his father's debts. Thea had been on to him about the need for Julia to come back and live with him – together with all the business of hiring a nanny. His sister had been a great help to him and now he was aware of having upset her. Even as children they'd never fallen out for more than a couple of hours. Now it seemed from Thea's urgent words on Sunday that she hadn't taken to Lacey and didn't want Richard to do anything he might regret.

Richard felt he owed Lacey an explanation for his sudden departure from Boston. If anyone had asked him a few weeks ago if he could see a future with her, he would've said yes. Now, seeing her in England, he wasn't so sure.

If he was honest with himself, meeting Emily, holding her in his arms for that brief time was what had knocked him off balance. He'd spent all weekend longing to see her again, just to prove to himself whether it was a true feeling or a heat of the moment mistake.

"Just tell me what needs doing, sweetie," cooed Lacey. "Leave it to me – I'll telephone the agency and find out what happened to that girl."

She reported back a short time later that the agency knew nothing either. Emily, it seemed, had vanished into thin air.

"That's strange." Richard felt hurt that she hadn't had the decency to tell him she wasn't coming back. It seemed out of character somehow.

Richard didn't find Lacey very easy to work with. Back in Boston she'd had a job in a clothes shop that she seemed to treat more like a drop in centre between beauty appointments than a place of work. Now, in his office, she sat on the corner of his desk, blocking the light when he was trying to put down some ideas for a project and spoiling his concentration.

Two things happened on Wednesday to break the tension that had been building inside Richard.

Lacey had investigated all the available hairdressers in Marchwood and found them all lacking. She finally found one in Worcester that sounded as if it might fit her exacting standards and had pestered Ginny to take her there.

Richard was thankful to have his office to himself. The vestiges of Lacey's cloying perfume still lingered, making him think of the lemon and coconut smell of Emily's hair and the smell of the incense she was burning that first morning and how stuffy she must have thought him when he told her to find some more suitable clothes.

Thinking of Emily reminded him that he needed to contact the agency again. If she wasn't coming back – and with each day that passed it looked increasingly doubtful – then he needed a replacement until Monica was fit to return to work.

The phone rang. He picked it up.

"Richard Kingsley. How can I help you?"

It was a young woman's voice and for an instant Richard felt hopeful it was Emily.

"This is a call for Lacey Tarlington," said the girl. "It's Camilla from *Brides Today* magazine. I forgot to ask her whether the wedding in August will be at the local church or at Marchwood Registry Office. Perhaps you can ask her to call me back."

Richard replaced the receiver in its holder and sat feeling numb. He didn't know whether he'd sat for hours or minutes. Lacey pushed open his office door and strolled in wearing a new outfit and smelling of expensive hairspray and perfume. She pirouetted in the middle of the room so he could get the full effect.

She stopped, as if she'd been freeze-framed.

"What's up Ritchie, what's happened?"

"I think you'd better sit down," he said. "I had a phone call from someone called Miranda at *Brides Today* magazine."

Lacey sat, her face an immaculate mask. "Well, what did she say?"

"Who are you marrying in August? How soon before the event would you have let me into the secret? A month? A week? The day before?" Richard's anger was white-hot. "I presume I was the one ear-marked to be the bride-groom? If not, let me be the first to congratulate the lucky man."

"Ritchie, don't be like that."

"And please stop calling me Ritchie. I don't like it."

"Sorry. Richard – I was going to propose to you before you left the States. I've been trying to get the words out ever so many times since I arrived here – but first there was Emily and then there was the complication with going to your sister's and collecting Julia."

"Julia is my daughter – she's not a complication. And don't you think you might have asked me first, before you start selling our story to the press?"

"I thought it might help you to keep your house," said Lacey. "I was only trying to help." She took a deep breath. "Look sweetie, you need the money to keep the house you love. If we marry then I'll get my grandfather's money."

"I'm not that desperate that I need to marry for money," said Richard.

"We'll see," said Lacey. "Think of what you might lose before you turn me down. I have a feeling that within a few hours you'll be saying you're prepared to accept my offer."

She flounced out and Richard heard her footsteps click-clacking down the stairs.

Richard's mobile bleeped. His heart sank. It was the accountant dealing with his father's affairs.

"Richard, we need to talk. Things look worse than previously anticipated. Despite my best efforts" – there was a dramatic pause – "it looks as if, unless a miracle happens, you will lose the house."

# CHAPTER NINE

Richard left the meeting with his accountant feeling that he might, after all, have no choice but to accept Lacey's proposal.

He heard his mother's voice in his head saying: *'Marry for love, not money. It's the only way you'll find true happiness.'*

He knew this was right, but true love would not clear the debts his father had left or enable his daughter to carry on living in the house that had been part of the Kingsley family for over two hundred years. Richard didn't want to go down in family history as the Kingsley who had lost Oakwood House.

He drove to the church where he and Helen had got married only seven years ago. He walked down the path and opened the heavy wooden door, entering into the cool interior that smelled of beeswax polish, musty hymn books and cold stone. Dust motes danced in a rainbow of light coming in through the stained glass window behind the altar.

Richard thought he'd never forget how Helen had looked on her wedding day. She carried a bouquet of deep pink roses and her grey eyes were full of love. The day felt as if it was painted with golden light and that feeling had only come to an end with her untimely death.

However, he stood by the altar steps trying and failing to visualise her face. He headed outside to her grave, feeling as if he had lead weights on his feet. The pale marble headstone in the shade of a yew tree gave her name and the dates of her birth and death, together with 'beloved wife of Richard Kingsley and mother of Julia Grace.'

He sat until a cloud blocked the sun and it began to drizzle. He went back to his car feeling as if he'd truly lost her now. The only face he could visualise was surrounded by dark curls and had eyes the colour of liquid amber.

Richard's next stop was the Agency.

Glenda looked flustered when he walked in. "Mr Kingsley – how can we help you?"

"Why didn't you let me know Miss Randall wasn't coming back? If there was a problem with working arrangements, why wasn't I consulted?" Richard stopped and took a deep breath. He hadn't realised how upset he was. The depression he'd suffered after Helen's death had crept up on him like that. One moment he was behaving normally and the next he was in the doctor's surgery being prescribed some little white pills.

"The instruction came from your office, Mr Kingsley."

"Well, it didn't come from me."

"Take a seat, Mr Kingsley. Just let me check your file and I'll tell you what happened." Glenda clicked a few keys on the computer.

Richard sat, trying not to fidget with impatience.

"Friday afternoon – an American lady from your office – a Miss Tarlington – called to say Emily's services were no longer required."

Richard thought Glenda had the triumphant look of a conjuror pulling a rabbit out of a hat.

"This was nothing to do with me," he said, "and I'd very much like her back. Where is she working at the moment? Can you give me her phone number?"

"I have no idea. She isn't employed by the Agency this week – and I'm sorry, we can't hand out personal information about our members of staff. Is there anything else I can help you with, Mr Kingsley?"

"Thank you – no," said Richard, remembering his manners.

He left the Agency and stood in the street for a few minutes uncertain of what to do next, aware that Glenda was watching him through the window.

Richard knew Emily needed money and he felt mad at Lacey for depriving her of the job – especially when she didn't really want to do it herself. He knew he should be concentrating on the bigger issue that involved sorting out the financial mess his father had left and finding practical solutions that would enable him to keep Oakwood House. He felt as if he was in one of those horror film scenes where the walls were closing in. Maybe Lacey's marriage idea would turn out to be his only option.

# CHAPTER TEN

It occurred to Richard that he did at least know where Emily lived. He told himself he just needed to put things right between them, ignoring the little voice in his head that suggested maybe there was more to it than that.

He drove towards the part of town where the old factories were and the rows of former workers' cottages surrounding them.

*"Second one in,"* she'd said the rainy night he'd dropped her back there with the rabbit.

He parked the car and headed towards the house, noting the sparkling white net curtains and the pathway edged with towering pink and yellow hollyhocks. The front gate creaked as he pushed it open and headed up the pathway towards the front door. He was seized with a moment of anxiety. What would he say to Emily? What if she didn't accept his apology for what had happened? What had he got to offer her? Richard almost turned away from the front door and headed back towards the safety of his car.

*"You've come this far, finish the job,"* he said to himself as he put his hand to the horseshoe shaped door knocker.

The sound echoed as if the house beyond was empty. He was about to turn away feeling a mixture of regret and relief. No – this wasn't good enough. He needed to at least let Emily know he'd tried to get in touch with her. He got one of his business cards out of his wallet and scribbled *'Sorry to have missed you'* on it and his initials. Would she interpret this as a romantic approach? How did he want her to view it?

He crouched down to put the card through the door and as he did so, he saw a figure lying crumpled on the hall floor. Richard had no idea if they were alive or dead.

At that point the lady next door came out of her front door and peered at him over the fence.

"Can I help you?" she asked. "Are you from the council? If so you need to be wary of Nelson. He doesn't like men very much." She had short iron-grey hair and a no nonsense manner that reminded Richard of his school librarian.

"I don't know about Nelson, but there's a lady on the floor in there who looks to be in a bad way," said Richard. "And no, I'm not from the council. My name's Richard Kingsley – I'm an architect."

"You call the emergency services, I'll get the spare key," said the lady. "My neighbour's name is Ada Brookes and she's just turned ninety. I'm Molly Bingham by the way – her next-door neighbour and occasional partner in crime." She looked friendlier now that he'd assured her he wasn't from the council.

Richard made the call on his mobile.

Molly returned with the key and she opened the front door. Richard was relieved to see that the lady was at least moving.

As he looked at her, there could be no doubt that Emily was related to her. The old lady had the same liquid amber eyes, but her face was framed with a cloud of silver hair, not Emily's dark curls.

"I knew you'd come back one day, Jack," she said, her face lighting up with a smile.

"I thought you said your name was Richard," said Molly, her face clouded with doubt.

"I did. It is."

Richard didn't have a chance to say any more. At that moment a yowling ball of ginger fur launched itself at his leg.

"Nelson doesn't like men," said Molly, shooing the irate cat into the utility room with the aid of her walking stick.

"Evidently," said Richard. "I remember Emily saying something about that."

"Molly, can you make Jack a cup of tea?" asked Ada. "I don't seem to be able to get up at the moment."

"Thank you – but I don't need tea," said Richard. He hoped the ambulance wouldn't be long.

Molly, who had done a first aid course, was busy getting Ada into the recovery position.

"Looks like you've got a bit of a bump on your head, love," she said. "What were you doing?"

A flash of blue lights outside signalled the arrival of the ambulance.

"I don't want no fuss," grumbled Ada. "I've got work to do. I can't be lying here answering a load of questions. My granddaughter will be back for her tea soon."

Molly and the ambulance crew persuaded her that she should go to hospital to be checked over properly.

"Well, I don't really feel myself," Ada conceded, "but I can't leave Emily to her own devices. Not at her age."

"I'll go and tell her," promised Richard, smiling to himself at the thought of Emily's response to this comment. "I'll bring her to the hospital to see you."

"Do you know where Emily's working?" he asked Molly.

"Yes – she's at the new café in the park. You can't miss it. It's bright pink."

After receiving assurances from the ambulance crew that Ada's injuries didn't seem to be too serious, Richard set off again.

He'd heard about the café in the park. Julia, who loved everything pink, had been in raptures about it earlier in the week at breakfast. Maria was equally enthusiastic. Richard, absorbed in his money worries, had taken little notice as the pair of them chattered on about the cakes and the big art table with the sequins and glitter.

He'd sat eating the bacon and eggs Ginny made for him and saying 'yes' and 'no' in the right places.

As usual, Lacey wasn't at breakfast. She stayed in bed as late as possible, showered, did her hair and make-up and then came downstairs where she would toy with a black coffee and some fresh fruit until it was time to leave. Richard was beginning to marvel that she wasn't stick thin and covered in wrinkles. She surely didn't eat enough to keep body and soul together. In America, she'd been the one encouraging him to eat something other than toast, to take regular exercise and stop drinking too much whisky. He hadn't noticed how severe her own regime was.

Richard reached the park and pulled up in the parking area near the swings. The café was close by, looking like a marshmallow on green jelly. A sign advertised 'All Day Breakfast £3.99' and 'Free coffee with every slice of chocolate cake.' A tantalising smell of frying bacon drifted towards him. He'd had two calls on his mobile – both from Andrew Crane about the financial situation.

"Some strange news has reached me from the Council Planning Department. I'm surprised you haven't discussed this with me." Andrew Crane's voice was like barbed wire scratching on a metal gate.

Richard smiled to himself. The financial advisor was like a caricature of the bird he was named after – long thin legs, a long thin nose with reading glasses perched at the end of them and a permanently disapproving expression. Everything he encountered was either 'strange', 'disturbing', 'surprising' or 'outrageous.' Richard had no idea what the man was talking about and he was in no hurry to find out.

He got slowly out of the car and headed towards the café trying to frame in his mind the words he needed to say to Emily.

He pushed open the café door and was enveloped in the fragrant, steamy warmth. He'd expected to see Emily behind the counter and was a little confused when he couldn't see her either there or through the double doors that swung open to the kitchen where a young girl was washing some dishes.

A woman with short blonde hair asked him what he would like.

Just as he was about to ask where Emily was, a flying object grabbed him around the legs for the second time that morning.

"Daddy, I told Maria it was you and she didn't believe me," said Julia. She had a dab of green paint on her face and her hands were spattered with yellow. Richard hoped there was none on his trousers.

"What are you doing here?" he asked.

“Daddy! We told you this morning. I could tell you weren’t listening.”

Richard swallowed a lump in his throat – Julia looked heart-breakingly grown up when she was telling him off, even down to the hands on her hips.

“Tell me again,” he said, not wanting to dampen her enthusiasm – the wish to find Emily uppermost in his mind.

“Come and see,” she said, dragging him by the hand. “This is my teacher, Emily. She’s very pretty.”

Emily’s reaction when she spotted Richard heading towards her was to run away. She could see by his face he was as shocked to see her as she was to see him. She assumed he’d just come to collect Julia and hadn’t expected her to be there.

She immersed herself in saying goodbye to the mothers and their children, making sure they’d got their pictures to take with them. She was thankful that this gave her something to do and was about to make some excuse to Angie and follow them out for a breath of fresh air.

Maria, after a whispered instruction from Richard, was about to leave with a paint-spattered Julia in tow.

The café had gone mysteriously quiet and Emily felt her heart racing and her legs go wobbly as Richard stood looking down at her.

“Aren’t you going with Julia and Maria?” she asked, aware that this probably sounded as if she didn’t want to talk to him.

“No – I came to find you.” His face was pale, his sea-green eyes focused on her face.

"Why? You made it perfectly clear you didn't want me to work for you anymore. I just wish you'd told me I wasn't suitable when you signed my time sheet." Emily's hurt feelings rushed out, despite the fact that she tried to keep them in check.

"That was a misunderstanding by someone else– but come along, bring your handbag and anything else you need. We're wasting time."

She looked at him questioningly. "What do you mean?"

Richard took a deep breath. "There's no easy way to tell you. Your grandmother is being taken to hospital. I thought you should know – that you'd want to be with her."

"What happened? Of course I want to be with her," said Emily, her eyes filling with tears.

"Come along then – my car's outside. I'll tell you as much as I know on the way."

Richard put a protective arm around Emily as he steered her towards the car. She leaned against him slightly and he worried in case she fainted again.

He started the engine and they headed from the car park into the stream of traffic going through the town centre towards the Worcester road.

"What happened? How do you know about Gran?"

"I found her. I'd called round to apologise for the misunderstanding about the job."

"Misunderstanding? You didn't want me anymore." Her eyes flashed amber fire.

"I did want you. Do want you," said Richard, trying to negotiate a tricky junction.

"So what happened then?"

"Lacey got the wrong end of the stick and told the Agency you weren't needed."

"Your fiancée was jealous in other words."

"She's not my fiancée."

"She seems to think she is."

A car overtook them, blasting its horn. Richard slowed down.

"Look," he said, "this isn't getting us anywhere. I called round to your house this morning to apologise as soon as I found out what had happened. That's when I discovered your grandmother."

Tears were pouring down Emily's face now – something Richard found harder to cope with than her flash of temper. "What's happened to her?"

"I didn't think you were going to ask," said Richard passing her his handkerchief.

He was rewarded with a faint smile as she dabbed at her eyes.

"It looked like she'd tripped coming down the stairs – she's got a bit of a bump on her head. She was saying a few odd things and the ambulance crew thought she ought to be checked over properly in hospital."

He didn't tell Emily they'd queried the possibility of a stroke. He didn't want to worry her.

"Thank you for being there and for coming to find me," said Emily. "Goodness knows what might have happened if she'd been left there until I got home tonight."

"I guess her cat might have dragged the lady next door round by the throat," said Richard. "He certainly is a fearsome beast."

"He didn't hurt you, did he? He doesn't like men very much."

"That's obvious," said Richard with a smile.

The waiting room of the A & E department was crowded when they arrived. The air smelled of antiseptic and trolleys and wheelchairs clattered in all directions, adding to the hubbub of noise. Nurses and doctors followed them looking frazzled. Names were called, people disappeared through doorways to be replaced by more people joining the long queue at the reception desk.

Emily stood, fidgeting from foot to foot, for what seemed hours anxious to know where her grandmother was.

Ada was in a side room. She was wearing a blue hospital gown and looked small and frail against the white pillow.

"Gran – you frightened me," said Emily rushing in and giving Ada a hug.

"Lot of silly nonsense dear," said Ada. "I told them, I was carrying a few bits and pieces down the stairs so I could wash them – and then the next minute I was at the bottom. You've been nagging me to get rid of those old slippers…"

"You should've left those things upstairs for me to carry down for you."

"Nonsense. How do you think I've managed all the time you've been gallivanting round London?"

"I'd have come and helped you if you'd needed me, you know that," said Emily.

"I know dear. And now those silly idiots are on about testing me to see if I've had a stroke. I told them I'm sure I haven't. I told that young man of yours he should just put me in my chair and leave me – but he would insist on calling an ambulance."

Emily flashed an apologetic grin at Richard who was hovering in the doorway.

At that moment a doctor arrived. "Hello Mrs Brookes. We're just going to run a few more tests."

"That's all you people want to do," complained Ada. "Poke at us like we're pincushions."

The doctor looked as if he'd heard all this before. "Pop back in about half an hour," he told Emily.

Emily gave Ada a kiss, reluctant to leave her. Out in the corridor, she gave way to tears again. She couldn't bear the thought of losing her beloved grandmother.

Richard was chafing at the need to get back to work. It seemed that a modified version of the library project would go ahead but he needed to do some serious work to keep things moving. However, his memories of the past combined with the current disturbance of Lacey coming back into his life made concentration difficult. He looked at Emily and his heart went out to her. It felt like only weeks since he'd stood alone in a corridor like this waiting for the news that would shatter his heart.

"Come along, we'll find a cup of coffee," he said to Emily.

She looked reluctant to move.

"You won't speed things up any by waiting outside the door. I'll give the doctor my mobile number and get him to call if they're finished sooner than expected."

She looked at him, eyes brimming. "It's just that I've got this idea of passing my strength on to her. She looks so tiny in that bed…"

Richard gave his phone number to a nurse who was going back into Ada's room. He was relieved when

Emily responded to the touch on her arm and walked with him along the corridor towards the canteen. They ordered coffee and slices of toast.

"I don't think I can eat anything," said Emily.

"Yes you can," he said, "and you must." He smiled at her. "I don't want you fainting on me again."

They sat at a table by the window that overlooked the car park. Emily sipped her coffee and looked at the toast.

"It's very easy," said Richard. "You pick it up and take a bite like this." He demonstrated. "Then you chew it and swallow it."

Emily followed his example, surprised to find that she was really hungry.

They talked about Julia and her passion for anything pink, the funny things she said and what good friends she and Rufus had become.

"She takes him for walks in her doll's pram," said Richard.

They skirted around the bigger subjects – Emily's lost gallery and failed romance, the loss of Richard's wife.

"Shouldn't you be at work?" Emily asked.

"Yes – but the thing with working for yourself is there's never an official finishing time. If necessary I'll go in later and put some hours in." He'd been thinking about doing this anyway. He and Lacey had been circling around each other like fencers and he had a terrible feeling he'd end up surrendering to her proposal. He thought of all the women in his family, going back into history, who had married for position or convenience. Why should he be any different? When he was in America he'd been so close to proposing to

Lacey. Why did she feel so wrong for him now he was back in England – and why did Emily feel so right?

Richard's mobile rang. He answered it and then passed the phone to Emily.

He watched as the expression on her face changed.

"Will she recover?" Emily's voice was cracked with emotion.

Richard fought the urge to draw her into his arms and kiss away the sadness on her face.

She ended the call and gave the phone back to Richard.

"What's happened?" he asked.

"She had a funny turn – they're not sure at the moment if it's shock from the bump on her head or a mini stroke. They've decided to keep her in."

"It's probably for the best," he said.

"She'll hate it. She's never been in hospital before. They're just moving her to Ward 12 and she's saying she wants to go home."

"Let's go and see her so you can convince her she needs to stay," said Richard.

They left the canteen and followed the signposts up some stairs and along a corridor until they found Ward 12.

They could hear Ada as soon as they'd rubbed the antiseptic gel on their hands and gone onto the ward. She was in another side room and making her views plain.

"You needn't bother about giving me a menu, I won't be staying for my tea. My granddaughter will be here in a minute to take me home. I haven't got time for this nonsense."

Richard and Emily smiled at each other as the quiet voice of a nurse tried to encourage and cajole without success.

"Emily – tell these people there's nothing wrong with me," said Ada as soon as she clapped eyes on her and Richard waiting near the doorway.

Emily sat by the bed and took Ada's hands in hers. She was aware suddenly of how frail Ada looked – almost child-like in the hospital bed. The amber fire in her eyes was still the same, though as she listed the things Emily needed to do for her.

"I'm supposed to be helping with the teas for the Floral Art Group tomorrow. Can you ask Molly if she can take my turn? And you'll need to make more of a fuss of Nelson. You know what he's like if I'm not there. He's as bad as you are for going off his food."

"Don't worry about anything, Gran. Just concentrate on getting better."

"There's nothing wrong with me," said Ada. "That's what I keep telling them."

If it hadn't been for the stab of fear in Ada's eyes, Emily might have believed her.

Emily managed to hold back the tide of emotion that swept through her until she'd left the ward. Richard was striding along next to her looking as if he was lost in his own thoughts. She remembered how he'd lost the wife he'd loved so dearly and wondered how she would cope if anything happened to Ada.

She stopped, fumbling in her handbag for a tissue to mop her streaming eyes.

Suddenly, Richard's arms were around her and she felt the comforting sensation of his heart beating against hers. The texture of his dark blue cotton shirt was soft against her face and she clung to him as if to a life-raft.

Long minutes passed before she became aware of people passing by, snatches of conversation, the rattle of wheel-chairs and trolleys and the faint smell of food over-riding the antiseptic smell as the evening meal was taken to the wards.

They stood locked together until a rumble of thunder sounded and they both looked out at the dark clouds that had gathered around the hospital like a purple blanket.

"Gran hates thunder," said Emily.

"Let's make a break for the car," said Richard.

They hurried along the corridor, her hand in his. It felt comforting.

They reached the safety of Richard's car before raindrops as big as two pence pieces began to fall. Emily fished her compact mirror out of her bag and did her best to wipe away her streaked mascara and dab at her reddened eyes.

"I'm sorry for being a problem to you again," she said. "I've never really thought about Gran dying before – and it's scary."

"You never expect the people you love best to die. When Helen died…" The sound of thunder and a flash of forked lightning masked Richard's last words.

He started the car hoping he could get back to Marchwood before the weather got worse. The rain eased temporarily, as if the storm was holding its breath, and then came back full force. The rain hammered on the roof of the car and bounced at least a foot up from the road. Within minutes, rivulets were running down the edges of the road. The windscreen wipers couldn't cope with the downpour even at full speed and visibility was poor.

Richard slowed down and turned off the main road.

"We need to stop somewhere until this is over."

Emily could barely hear him over the crash of the thunder and the jagged scarring of the lightning. The trees that edged the road were swaying to a violent rhythm and the light had faded from the sky.

Richard pulled into the car park of a little country pub with black and white beams. Emily could just make out the name 'The Country Girl' on the frantically swinging sign.

"My parents used to bring us here," said Richard. "Beyond that curtain of rain is an orchard and Thea and I had great fun there in the autumn scrumping apples and looking for frogs in the pond."

He'd parked as close as possible to the solid wooden door of the pub. The lights were on inside and a sign proclaimed it was open although there were very few cars in the car park.

"This looks set for a while," said Richard. "We may as well stop for a bite to eat."

Emily opened her mouth to protest.

"Their speciality here is goulash – they have a Hungarian chef. It would be rude not to stay and try it."

He got out of the car and came round to the passenger side to open the door for her.

"Make a run for the doorway," he said, pausing the lock the car.

The pub had low ceilings, oak beams and a tantalisingly spicy smell drifted from the kitchen where a foreign voice was raised in song. They sat in an alcove with red velvet seats.

"Goulash, then?" asked Richard.

Emily fumbled in her bag. "I haven't got much money on me."

"Don't worry about that."

"But – you need money so you can keep your house." Emily flushed scarlet, feeling she'd said more than she should.

"The price of a couple of bowls of goulash won't make any difference."

Emily noticed how his jaw looked tense and she wished she'd kept her mouth shut.

Richard went to order two small bowls of goulash and two glasses of red wine. He brought back an information sheet about the chef who had arrived at the pub several years ago penniless and only able to cook goulash. The pub owner, whose regular chef had just quit in a fit of temper, was grateful for any help and asked him to stay until he could find a reliable replacement.

"He's still here, fifteen years on," said Richard, "and still making goulash."

Emily made a mental note to tell Nick about this place. She had a feeling he'd find it as fascinating as she did. She checked her mobile phone. No news.

"If there's a problem they will call you," said Richard. "Now, relax and drink your wine."

Richard had sent a text to Ginny saying he'd been unexpectedly delayed and wouldn't need any dinner. He hadn't replied to any of Lacey's messages wanting to know where he was.

Their food arrived, the white bowls of goulash accompanied by chunks of crusty bread.

"If this is a small bowl, I dread to think what the large one is like," said Emily.

"It's about the size of a washing up bowl," said Richard picking up his spoon.

They finished their food and a look outside confirmed that the rain had stopped.

"Maybe we should go," said Emily, reluctantly. "You've got work to do and I feel guilty keeping you away from it. I need to tell Molly about Gran so she can tell the Floral Art Group, not to mention making sure Nelson doesn't get malnutrition."

"If that's the creature that savaged my leg, I don't think there's much danger of it," said Richard.

They lingered over coffee before venturing out into the car park. The ground was full of puddles that reflected clouds turning pink in the evening light. In the orchard, the apples and plums hung on the trees like Christmas decorations and the grass was starred with raindrops.

The scent of elderflower surrounded them from a tree not far from where Richard's car was parked. They both moved slightly to make sure they weren't showered by damp petals. Emily lost her footing and stumbled. Richard caught her arm to steady her. Then his arms went round her and their lips met in a kiss.

Emily's stomach felt as if she'd gone down too fast in a lift. They pulled away, looking at each other as if neither of them could believe what had happened. Richard looked as if he was about to say something but his mobile bleeped with an incoming text and the mood was broken.

"He stared at the small screen as if he couldn't understand the words on it."

"Bad news?" asked Emily softly.

"I don't know. It's my sister. I'll call her when I get home."

They drove in silence past damp hedgerows, finally reaching the wider roads and buildings that signified the approach to Marchwood. He dropped Emily outside Ada's house. There was an awkward silence when he stopped the car.

"Thank you," said Emily.

"Call me if I can help."

"You've done more than enough already."

Richard watched as she went through the gate next door to Ada's and knocked on the front door of the neighbour's house. His heart ached for her. He knew what it was like to be worried about losing somebody – and if something did happen, the bus service was poor and she didn't have a car.

Emily came out of Molly's house and waved goodbye. Richard drove off feeling a sense of dread as to why Thea needed to speak to him so urgently.

# CHAPTER ELEVEN

Thea answered the phone immediately, as if she'd been waiting for it to ring.

"Where on earth have you been, Richard?"

He didn't have a chance to reply – she just rattled on in typical Thea style. Usually she was very direct when she needed to say something. This time he got the feeling she was circling round the subject, unsure of what to say.

"You've had Andrew Crane on the phone," he said to her. "What did he want? Why didn't he call me?"

"He tried, we've all tried, but nobody could get hold of you. Where have you been?"

"Helping a friend with a relative in hospital."

"It's not like you to go anywhere near a hospital if you don't have to," said Thea. The words '*since Helen*' crackled, unspoken, between them.

"There was nobody else."

"Richard – you're not losing yourself again are you?" This was a kind of shorthand between them for the state he'd been in after he'd lost Helen.

"No, I think I'm finding myself again."

"Are you going to marry Laccy?"

The direct question stunned him. "I might have no choice if I want to keep the house."

"Mother always said it was wrong to marry without love."

"I don't want to go down in history as the Kingsley who lost Oakwood House."

"Andrew Crane had some strange news. I asked him if he'd been drinking but he assured me he hadn't."

"What sort of news?" Richard's head was aching and he still had work to do on the revised designs.

"Do you know anything about planning permission for a theme park at Oakwood House?"

"Are you sure you haven't been drinking, Thea? What are you talking about?"

"Talk to Andrew Crane. He's got all the details."

It was only when Emily was in Molly's cluttered sitting room she realised she hadn't thanked Richard properly for the help he had given her today. The atmosphere between them on the journey back to Marchwood had been fragile as cobwebs and he'd seemed unsettled, as if impatient for her to be gone. She'd whispered a brief 'goodbye and thank you' and hurried off. She was therefore surprised to see him still sitting there in his car when she came out of Molly's house to go back to Ada's.

When he saw her, he'd driven off, his face looking pale against the dark interior of the car.

Molly had a lot to say about Richard.

"So who is this new boyfriend of yours?"

"He's not my boyfriend."

"Are you sure he didn't have something to do with your Gran's accident?" Molly was a great fan of murder mysteries. "It seems a bit fishy that he arrived at about the same time."

"He came looking for me."

Molly was like a steam-roller. "And all that calling himself one name and then another. He said his name was Richard and yet Ada was calling him Jack."

Something stirred a memory with Emily but she couldn't pin down what it was.

"He's Richard Kingsley from Oakwood House – and he's already spoken for," she said, trying to act as if she didn't care.

# CHAPTER TWELVE

Emily spent a restless night. She wished Nelson was the sort of cat who would be cuddled but he was, as usual, out on the prowl.

At six o'clock, she gave up any pretence of being able to sleep. She'd lain awake for hours thinking about the hours she'd spent with Richard – how natural it had felt to be in his arms and how perfect it would have been if it hadn't been for Ada lying in hospital and not knowing what was going to happen to her.

She got up and dressed, went downstairs and put some food down for Nelson. He came through the cat flap at six thirty and gave her a baleful stare, clearly annoyed at things being done in the wrong order. He went and sniffed at Ada's chair and looked up at Emily as if asking where she was. This made Emily cry again and she picked up Nelson and cuddled him anyway.

Emily didn't bother with breakfast – she didn't think she'd be able to swallow anything. It was too early to phone the hospital. She headed towards the café. Angie had given her a spare key.

"I'm hopeless with them," she said. "At least if we've both got one then we stand a chance of being able to get in."

By the time Angie arrived, Emily was well into painting another mystical tree. She was using shades of blue and grey with touches of silver – inspired by yesterday's thundery skies, the colour of Richard's shirt and the silver that edged the clouds when the sun came out.

"So what happened yesterday? I didn't like to keep texting you. It looked as if you were in good hands."

"Richard was very kind," said Emily, a flush staining her cheeks.

"I see," said Angie, her mouth twitching in amusement. "It looks as if you might be giving Miss America some serious competition."

"I don't think so." Emily's heart said otherwise. Now that she'd been distracted from painting her senses vibrated with the memory of being in Richard's arms.

"So how is Ada?"

"It's the usual story from the hospital. She's had a 'comfortable night' and they're running more tests." Emily's face crumpled. "I'm so worried about her."

"What would she say if she was here now?" asked Angie, who had become familiar with Ada's sayings over the years.

Emily brushed away the tears on her eyelashes. "She'd say I should get on with something positive – that no amount of worry would change anything to do with your fate."

"Exactly," said Angie. "Tea and toast coming up. I bet you've not had any breakfast."

There was an excited glow about Angie that Emily couldn't ignore. It was more than the café taking off and doing well. Emily heard her on the phone later that morning. Angie had gone into the kitchen to sort a list for the wholesale supplier. She'd been longer than usual and Emily had broken off from her painting to take the orders from people queueing at the counter.

Angie looked flushed and excited as she finished the call. Her giggle bubbled like the cry of a curlew as she said goodbye.

*'Definitely not a supplier,'* thought Emily and waited to find out who had put the sparkle back into her friend's eyes.

At that moment a group of cyclists came in, hungry for bacon sandwiches and coffee. Emily washed her hands and came to help Angie clear tables and sort cutlery.

It was nearly lunchtime by the time Angie was able to tell Emily the good news.

"Nick rang earlier to say that his article is in today's 'Guardian.' On the way here I called into the newsagents and bought several copies." She indicated a canvas bag stuffed full of newspapers.

"Let me see." Emily scanned the article feeling excited for her friend.

"He's got some great stuff in about you too," said Angie. "He mentions what a great artist you are and the events we're running here."

There was a photo of the two of them either side of one of Emily's paintings together with an array of Angie's tempting cakes.

Angie made tea for them. "It was really funny in the newsagents. The lady on the counter said 'do you know these are all the same newspaper?' and I said that my café was featured in it. She looked at me as if I was completely crazy – but it did some good because a few people in the queue asked for my contact details and said they'd be in touch."

"So I suppose you and Nick will be arranging another celebration then," said Emily.

"I suppose we will," said Angie with a broad smile as she headed back towards the kitchen.

# CHAPTER THIRTEEN

Richard arrived home after he'd dropped Emily off, expecting an inquisition from Lacey, to find that she'd gone to London and would be back sometime the following day.

Ginny emerged from the kitchen looking harassed. Andrew Crane had left several messages, Lacey had been foul-tempered because she couldn't get hold of Richard before she left for London. Julia had asked constantly where Daddy was and Maria hadn't known what to do with her.

Richard made some excuses about being out of town and the mobile reception being non-existent. He wasn't sure if she believed him. At that moment his mind was too full of Emily and not wanting to leave her to be able to think of anything else. He wished he'd said more before she left him about seeing her again, but he hadn't known what to say.

He went to his study, took out his phone and scrolled back through the messages Lacey had sent him yesterday. She kept referring to a previous message she'd sent him which he didn't have.

Richard forced himself to stay awake until he'd completed the proposed revisions to the designs he was working on. By the time he finished and decided to go to bed, everyone else in the house was asleep. He'd drunk so much strong coffee to keep awake, he was now jittery and unable to relax. He'd been unable to contact Andrew Crane and worries about further bad news circulated in his tired mind on an endless track.

He gave up the pretence of trying to sleep and got up, pulled back the curtains and sat on the window-seat he'd loved since he was a child. He slept in what used to be his parents' bedroom and the window-seat overlooked the park and the places he used to play as a child. He'd thought he'd always have this to hand on to his children, and felt sad to think this probably wouldn't happen unless he accepted Lacey's proposal.

The next morning, he went downstairs before it was light feeling gritty-eyed and exhausted. Ginny, who was always an early riser gave a start as if she'd seen a ghost when she saw him sitting at the kitchen table with a mug of tea and some toast.

"Couldn't you wait for breakfast?" she asked with a smile.

"I couldn't sleep."

When he went into the sitting room, he was horrified to see that some drastic changes had been made. The silver framed photos on top of the polished table, including his wedding photo and those of baby Julia, had been removed and replaced by one of Richard and Lacey taken in Boston. The dark green and pink patchwork cushions Helen had made had been replaced by plain cream satin ones that did nothing for the room. A few items of furniture, including the maroon footstool his mother had always used, had gone.

He called Ginny. "Who's been messing about with this room?"

Ginny flushed. "It was Miss Tarlington's idea to change a few things."

"Well, why didn't you stop her? Where is everything?"

"Mr Kingsley, as you well know, I'm just the hired help." There was an edge to Ginny's voice that he hadn't heard before. "And I have to tell you that if you go ahead with your plans I won't be the hired help much longer."

"What plans?"

"Your plans to marry Miss Tarlington."

"I haven't agreed to anything of that kind yet."

"She obviously thinks you have. She's gone to London for a wedding dress fitting."

"Just tell me where everything is and I'll put it back where it belongs. I'll take full responsibility for my actions." Richard didn't know why he'd said that. Oakwood House was his at the moment – he could have the rooms as he wished.

"It's all upstairs in the spare room," said Ginny. She said something about a photo shoot. She was very secretive about it."

Richard piled up the cream satin cushions in the corner of the room. "You can take these to the nearest charity shop," he said.

"Charity shop?" queried Ginny.

"Yes – I do know about them."

"But I think these were expensive."

"Then they've hit the jackpot, haven't they?"

He headed up the curved staircase with the intention of bringing the photos down but he got waylaid by Julia who shot out of her bedroom like a bullet from a gun. She was fully dressed, although she hadn't managed to do up the buttons at the back of her dress, and had clearly been down the stairs to scrounge a biscuit from Ginny.

"Daddy! Where did you go yesterday? What happened to Emily? Her picture's in the paper today. Ginny told me. I'll show you when we go downstairs. Why did you go off in your car with her? "Where did you go? Did you go for a picnic?" She wrapped her arms round his right leg, making walking any further impossible. He sank down on the faded blue landing carpet that had been there since before he was born and gathered her onto his lap. She put her arms round his neck and he could smell the newly washed cotton of her pink summer dress.

Maria emerged, rubbing her eyes.

"*Buongiorno* – Good morning Mr Kingsley. Julia that is enough questions for your Daddy. Let him answer – and let him breathe."

Julia relaxed her grip, but the torrent of questions didn't stop.

"Daddy – you promised one day we'd go for a walk and look for deer tracks in the woods. Will it be today? Please?"

"Just a very quick walk then," he said, "and then I must go to work."

Julia ran to fetch her trainers and Maria, still yawning, helped her to put them on.

"Lacey was very cross yesterday when you didn't come home." Julia's monologue continued whether Richard answered or not. "She stamped her foot like this."

A smile crossed Maria's face as she went to fetch a cardigan for Julia.

Julia was excited to have some special time with her Daddy. She'd been happy yesterday at the art workshop in the café that did the special biscuits with the chocolate chips in. She loved the story Emily told about the princess who'd escaped from a wicked queen and ended up having to eat some magic strawberries so that she could shrink small enough to get into a special hiding place under the roots of an oak tree. Emily had shown them what the leaves of an oak tree looked like and they'd painted leaves and made prints of them on their pictures.

She told Daddy about her picture as they went down the staircase and out through the doors that led from the sitting room to the garden. They went out and saw Rufus and Julia fed him and talked to him. Julia promised she'd take him out in the dolls pram later.

Julia had wanted to go and look at the place her Daddy called the folly, but it seemed he had other ideas today. They went into the woods and had fun collecting leaves and Daddy was very impressed because Julia knew what an oak tree looked like and he said when she was bigger he'd teach her to climb that one. She wondered why he looked sad when he said it and why they headed home for breakfast soon after.

When they got back, Julia helped him carry the photos and cushions back to the sitting room. It took ages because Julia wanted to know who the people were and Richard tried to weave little stories around the pictures. She especially liked the ones of her mother.

"She was very pretty wasn't she Daddy?"

"So are you sweetheart," he said, a lump coming to his throat.

Julia had loved being with Emily yesterday and wished the class could have gone on longer. She thought Maria had liked it too. The added bonus was when Daddy arrived and she'd hoped they could have all stayed and played in the park. But Daddy had his serious face on and he'd asked Maria if she could take Julia home. He had to go somewhere with Emily.

Julia didn't understand where they had to go. She asked Daddy about it and he told her about Emily's grandmother and how she was now in hospital. Julia couldn't remember her grandmothers. They'd both died when she was small. It must be nice to have one you could live with and do things with.

Lacey had been on the phone again when Julia had got home. She'd looked up expectantly but her gaze fell when she saw just Julia and Maria.

"Where is your Daddy?" she'd asked, her voice scratchy as barbed wire.

"He's gone somewhere with Emily," said Julia. She noticed how Lacey's silvery eyes flashed like the wicked queen's in a Disney film she'd once seen.

Ginny called them into the dining room for lunch. Lacey spent a long time picking at a few lettuce leaves and totally ignoring the tuna mayonnaise rolls Ginny had made. She sipped at her mineral water and glared at Julia just like a witch in a fairy-tale casting a spell.

Julia wondered if she should have mentioned about Daddy and Emily.

Richard was surprised how moved he felt walking across the lawn and into the trees with Julia, her hand in his. The main thought running through his mind was that, whatever happened, this might be one of the last occasions like this they had together.

He looked back at the solid, square shape of the house gleaming white in the early morning sun and felt weary at the thought of how much packing there would be to get rid of everything and move from here. There must be stuff in the attics going back to when the house was built.

Thea had suggested opening the place to the public but the cost of getting enough health and safety stuff in place was prohibitive and besides there wasn't enough of interest to draw many people.

He would have liked to renovate the folly. It was his grandmother's favourite place to sit and she always said it was a special place. She told the children made up stories about it - she always said she'd seen ghosts there. Even though Richard and a friend had camped out near it one autumn night, all they'd done was get cold and damp with a mist that had come down. The only thing they'd seen was an owl that had hooted for most of the night and kept them awake. His grandmother had claimed when she was an old lady that she'd seen anything from a Roman centurion to Oliver Cromwell, but she was getting dementia by then so nobody took any notice.

He told himself he should stop thinking about Emily even though his heart was screaming at him to phone her. He should do, he told himself, just to find out how her grandmother was.

Three things stopped him from doing so that day.

When he got back from the walk with Julia it was to the news that Andrew Crane was waiting for him in his study. Crane, who always reminded Richard of the bird he was named after with his long thin legs and pointed nose was pacing up and down the small room just like something in captivity.

"There you are, Kingsley," he said. "I wondered when you might decide to return."

The expression on his face was severe, making his nose look sharper than ever. He had a copy of the local newspaper with him which he placed on the desk in front of Richard.

"This is going to do your cause no good at all," he said, pointing at the offending article with a long finger. "No good at all."

The black banner headline read: 'Local landowner set to destroy wildlife.'

There followed an outline of what Richard planned to do – and the fact that money was coming from America.

"But none of this has come from me," protested Richard.

"There may have been a way of turning things round- but not now you've stirred up The Wildlife Trust."

"But what exactly are they accusing me of?" None of this made any sense to Richard.

Andrew Crane stared at him as if he was a complete idiot.

"I gather you are to marry Miss Lacey Tarlington."

Richard began a stumbling explanation that he'd agreed to no such thing yet. Andrew Crane held up his hand for silence.

"It seems that Miss Tarlington's father is keen for the marriage to go ahead – and that there is a considerable amount of money involved should it do so. The pay-off where Clive Tarlington is concerned is that he will erect a small theme park on your land. I gather they are small affairs, more like giant puzzles than ferris wheels and designed to match their setting. He has one near Paris, I believe, with the theme of the French Revolution." He paused for dramatic effect. "This is in the small print of the agreement between you and Miss Tarlington and naturally her father has taken steps to obtain planning permission so that the work may be completed as quickly as possible."

"But I don't like theme parks."

"Somebody obviously thinks you do – and the local conservation groups are threatening to stage a sit-in on the main road to prevent the bulldozers coming in to begin work."

"Who gave them the story in the first place?"

"How many journalists do you know? The report says 'a reliable source.' To whom have you spoken about your financial situation?"

Richard shook his head. His family and the people he lived with were obviously aware of his circumstances. He made a list in his head – Thea and her husband Mark (not their style), Maria (English too poor), Lacey (unlikely) and Ginny who had always been totally loyal to the Kingsley family.

He remembered her spark of irritation when she'd talked about being the hired help. The only other face that came into his mind was Emily's. She would do anything to protect wildlife – but how would she have found out about the theme park plans. She and the friend she worked in the café with had clearly spoken to a journalist. What if he'd wormed more out of Emily than she realised – or was one of those under-cover investigative reporters?

Andrew Crane sat with his long fingers steepled together. "Well, if it isn't true, I think you'll have to get the paper to print an apology. Let's hope you don't get too many people snooping around in the meantime."

Richard didn't say anything. He felt sick at the thought of everything he'd loved since he was a boy being disrupted and ruined by a theme park, no matter how small and tasteful it was. If that was one of the terms and conditions of marriage to Lacey, then he definitely didn't want it, even if it meant losing Oakwood House. Then the thought occurred to him that if he ended up having to sell, Clive Tarlington would snap up the property at the lowest possible price, without the need to marry off his daughter.

After Andrew Crane had gone, Richard sat gazing out of the window hoping to find inspiration and a way forward out of this mess.

Richard knew he needed to see Emily again – not just to reassure himself that she had nothing to do with any of this. Julia's comment about Emily being in the paper today stirred his mind.

He went to ask Ginny, who was doing the ironing, if this was true. Ginny was working in what had once been the old scullery. The smell of clean cotton and lavender spray conflicted with the smell of damp and bleach. Folded sheets were draped over an indoor washing line and shirts hung ghost-like on the doors and chairs.

"I remember Miss Randall," said Ginny. "The pretty young lady who had a funny turn and was so appreciative of my fruitcake." This was a barbed criticism of Lacey who found fault with everything to do with food and so frustrated Ginny. "Julia noticed her photo in The Guardian. It seems she's a very talented artist. It's an article about that café in the park – fancy that getting a mention in a newspaper like The Guardian."

Richard read the article, remembering some of the things Emily had told him yesterday. Seeing her photo reminded him of the feeling of her in his arms and the kiss they had shared yesterday in the busy hospital corridor. He wondered if it had meant as much to her as it had to him – whether she too felt as if the ground under her feet was unsteady. So much of his own feelings had been tied up in memories of Helen's last moments of life – the moment the doctor came to say there was no further hope and the way he was unable to absorb that knowledge and just kept sitting there, her hand in his. It was as if being back in the antiseptic atmosphere had brought all that back – together with the emptiness of knowing he would have to go through the rest of his life without the woman he'd loved for so long.

Richard had met Helen at Art College. He'd gone to study design and, by the second year had decided to change and do architecture. She had also had a change of heart and, following a visit to the American Museum in Bath had come back with a passion for textiles. She'd experimented in her spare time and had ended up buying a second hand sewing machine and developing her own small business before she left the college. People said some of the quilts she made were like paintings and hung them on walls rather than putting them on beds or sofas.

He noticed that Emily had the same passion for colour. The painting she was working on when he saw her the previous day reminded him of an evening sunset when he and Helen were on their honeymoon in Cornwall and the sun had set in a riot of pink, orange and gold over the sea. They lay together in their four-poster bed just watching until the last vestiges of light disappeared over the horizon and the first stars appeared.

A quote from a poem that Thea had given him after Helen died returned to him now and finally meant something. "A part of our love will be in every sunrise and sunset and will never die."

# CHAPTER FOURTEEN

For the first time in her life, things were not going Lacey's way. She couldn't see what the big deal was about needing so much planning permission for a small theme park on what would soon be her land.

"You need to be patient, honey," her father said a few days ago. "I'll sort it as soon as I can."

"But I could lose the deal with *'Brides Today'* magazine," wailed Lacey.

"I take it Richard is happy with everything?"

"Sort of." Lacey felt like she had when she was in seventh grade and she'd been caught cheating in a science test. A letter had been sent home to her father and she could still feel the weight of his steel-eyed glare as she traced a pattern on the carpet with her toe.

"Sort the basics first," he said. "What if he knocks your offer back?"

"He won't."

"Don't count your chickens, honey."

Once again, he'd made her feel like a grubby seventh grader. She wished she'd been more positive when Richard was in Boston and had engineered a proposal then. She'd been so sure he was the one for her. Now, in England, she felt this certainty crumbling.

As much as anything, she wanted her father to notice her on equal terms and to treat her as a partner with the first of his mini theme parks to be created in England. She felt it would improve her status amongst the half-brothers and sisters her father had placed her amongst as a result of his many marriages.

Lacey wanted to be the centre of attention. She wanted her wedding in England to be the social event of the year, a dream that was fading fast because she hadn't realised before that despite having a big house and a lot of land, Richard wasn't a member of the aristocracy and Oakwood House was in desperate need of a make-over. She'd made a start with a few superficial changes to the sitting room, despite the fact that the housekeeper had acted as if she'd committed the crime of the century. If she thought that was bad then Lacey wondered how she'd react when they started work on the theme park. She refused to say 'if.'

She felt it could only be a good thing. There was altogether too much green space around the house which made her feel uncomfortable. The theme park would only take up a field or two and would be an unusual interpretation of some English fairy-tales using a mixture of secret passages, mind games, holograms and music. Apart from the famous one in Paris, her father had placed a 'mountain adventure' theme park near one of the ski resorts in Vermont but his aim was to have one in every country in Europe.

Lacey had big plans for after the wedding. She intended for Oakwood House to become one of the most visited places in England – and imagined herself being photographed frequently by the glossy magazines she so loved reading.

Yesterday, she'd headed down to London on the train, thankful she'd paid extra for a first class ticket. She had things to do – a fitting for the wedding dress she'd seen online in an exclusive shop – and a meeting with an estate agent to talk about available property. She had no intention of spending her life buried in the countryside. On the train she scanned the details of apartments overlooking the Thames and thought of nights in London going to shows and fancy restaurants.

She was glad Richard hadn't been around yesterday to question where she was going. He'd put up a brittle façade around her since she'd arrived. Lacey was so sure he still needed her to make the decisions for him. Look what a mess he'd been when he first came to Boston. Under her protection he'd produced great work and they'd had a good social life. There had always been that air of British reserve about him and when someone had told her about him losing his wife, she'd not felt able to push him.

She'd been surprised by his sudden departure and also by how much she missed him. Having followed him to England she'd realised she wasn't a moment too soon when she saw him with Emily and realised his heart wasn't as frozen as she'd been led to think. This had made her more determined than ever to marry him herself.

It was her friend Glenda who had urged caution. Glenda knew the best and the worst of her. It was Glenda she'd phoned from London to tell her about the fitting for her wedding dress – how much the elaborate gown was costing and how many beads and crystals were hand-sewn onto it.

"So is it Richard you care about or is it the opportunity to turn your life into a soap opera that's the attraction."

"Of course I care about him," she'd stormed back, startling the people sitting near her in the elegant café where she was having mint tea and a celebratory hand-made chocolate.

"I don't think you're being honest with yourself," said Glenda.

"You're just jealous."

"You've always been attention seeking. It's always about you. It doesn't sound as if you've considered Richard or anybody else in this new drama of yours."

Lacey had ended the call and gone and sat in a cubicle in the Ladies, leaning her head against the cool tiles on the wall. Well, if that was Glenda's attitude, she'd not bother to tell her anything else.

On the train, she ran through the previous day's events in her mind. She'd gone for the fitting for the dress, surprised at how heavy it was and how tight the corset underneath felt, despite the way she'd watched everything she ate since coming to England very carefully and hadn't put on any weight.

"One has to suffer to be beautiful," said the sales assistant.

Lacey had expected to feel a sense of magic when she first put the dress on and was bewildered to find she didn't feel anything. The shop had a tasteful window with only two gowns in the window. The inside was tastefully decorated with filigree silver and white lights and smelled expensive. The fitting room, where she was given a glass of champagne, had carpets where you sank up to your ankles. There were delicate looking chairs and mirrors cunningly placed to show the bride and her attendants to best advantage.

The black-clad sales girls were silent as stage crew as they fetched and carried, assisted with fitting and made suggestions for improvement.

"You could have brought your mother or a friend," said one of the women.

"I prefer to do this myself," said Lacey. She knew what her mother's attitude and Glenda's would be to a place like this. '*You could feed a poor family for two years on what you're paying for that dress.*'

And her mother – *'The best thing you can do, girl, is get yourself a job.'* Her mother, of whom Lacey was bitterly ashamed, who had turned her back on her husband's money and started her own cleaning business. She'd had the nerve to offer Lacey a job! Lacey had no intention of doing any more work than she could help.

She'd shut down those voices as she finished the fitting, paid the bill and arranged for delivery by courier once a few minor alterations were done, and headed to Claridges where she was spending the night.

Now on the crowded train from Paddington those voices intruded again. Waking up this morning, she'd felt the loss of Glenda's friendship. She'd always begun each day by texting her brief details of what was going on. Her friend was not responding.

She thought back to the terrible lunch at Richard's sister's house and how he'd told everyone about the rabbit he'd got for Julia to play with when they got home.

"Where did you get it from?" Thea had asked.

"Emily – my temporary secretary – rescued him from a shop that was closing down." His eyes had softened when he said Emily's name in a way they never did when he looked at Lacey.

Lacey sat on the train as it rattled and swayed across Oxfordshire farmland. Emily – was a thorn in her side. Emily who bought clothes in charity shops and who rescued cute furry animals. Emily who gave the impression of being weak and fragile but underneath was more than capable of wrecking Lacey's plans.

The train stopped at Oxford and several people in her carriage got out. A man walked past her, dropping his copy of The Guardian on the empty seat beside Lacey.

She almost told the man to take his trash with him, but her attention was caught by something on the page the newspaper was turned to. Lacey snatched up the paper and scanned the photos on it. Emily and a blonde woman in what looked like a café smiling happily at whoever was behind the camera.

Even in the black and white photos, Emily had a beauty and exuberance that money couldn't buy and Lacey felt a worm of jealousy turn in her stomach. She remembered as she was going off to the station, Julia's excited return from the art group at the pink café. She was clutching a gaudy painting that was covered in what looked like leaf prints and a liberal coating of silver glitter that was cascading onto the kitchen floor.

"Julia, look at the mess you're making." Lacey was aware she had spoken sharply but there was no need for the child's bottom lip to wobble in a way that indicated tears would soon follow.

"Don't worry about it. That's easily swept up," said Ginny the housekeeper bustling in with yet another plateful of calorie-laden sandwiches. You can't have a painting without glitter can you Julia?"

Lacey noticed how Julia's expression changed from rain to sunshine in an instant, something that proved to her that the child was manipulative.

As the train journey progressed, the worm of jealousy inside Lacey grew and squirmed. She'd not taken any notice of what the child said about her teacher at the art class. Lots of children thought their teachers were wonderful. Then, when Richard hadn't arrived back as expected, Julia had said the words that made Lacey fume with silent rage.

*"Daddy's gone somewhere with Emily."* There was a smirk on Julia's face as if she knew how much those words would act like acid in Lacey's jealous heart.

When the train reached Marchwood, Lacey waited impatiently for a taxi. She'd originally intended to go back to Oakwood House and ask Richard what was going on – but now she had a better idea.

"Can you drop me by the café at the park and wait for me while I deliver a message to somebody?" she asked the taxi driver.

"As long as you don't keep me waiting too long, lady," he said, staring up at her without getting out of his cab. "I got one of me regulars to take to the hairdressers at eleven thirty. Where do you want to go after that?"

"Oakwood House."

"The one with all the kerfuffle in the paper?" He looked at her. "You're not one of those papparazi types are you? If so I don't want to get caught up in nothing…"

"I don't know what you're talking about," she said briskly. "Now do you want the job or not?"

"OK, OK," he got out of his car, grumbling, unlocked the boot and stashed her large suitcase into it. "Been away for a fortnight, have yer?" he asked, puffing with exertion.

"No, just overnight."

## CHAPTER FIFTEEN

Emily was sitting in the café working on an idea for an adult and child series of cookery workshops. She'd sketched some ideas for characters who could feature in little stories built around the recipes.

She had to keep breaking off to help Angie because Charlene, the girl who'd been coming in to help over lunchtimes and afternoons, hadn't arrived yet.

"That's a great idea," said Angie. "Storytime with food. Maybe you could create recipe cards that customers could take away?"

Emily ate a simple lunch of boiled eggs and Marmite toast, happily scribbling ideas in her sketchbook. She was feeling happier because Angie had taken her to see Ada last night and the news had been good.

"They're going to let me home tomorrow," said Ada, providing the doctor's still happy." She looked around. "Mind you, it's not as if they've done much other than try to make out I'm past my sell by date."

Angie and Emily had laughed at this. "You're in better condition than some of the nurses," Angie had said.

Emily had shut the events in London that ended with James's betrayal behind a door in her mind. Ada had urged her to move on from whatever disappointment she'd had. Emily still hadn't been able to tell her grandmother everything that had happened and she wondered if she ever would totally trust anyone again.

Richard had set her heart racing on a few occasions but she knew better than to trust the feelings he'd aroused, no matter how good he'd been to her. She was happy that today, for the first time since James had let her down, her ideas were flowing freely. She thought it was probably because of the article in The Guardian.

Angie was excited because of the interest it had already aroused. Someone from the local paper had been in touch and Nick had sent a text to say that one of the glossy county magazines also wanted to do an article.

"I can't believe how well things are going," she said.

Her phone rang and her expression changed. "Thanks for letting me know." Her voice was clipped.

"What's up?"

"That was Charlene's mother to say she won't be in today – or ever – because she's got another job. *'She felt you expected a lot of her and she was on her feet a lot.'* What did she expect – it's a café."

"Why couldn't she phone you herself?"

"Good question. I bet she decided not to come because she knows we've got that W I group in for cream teas."

Angie picked her phone up and keyed in a number.

"What are you doing?"

"I'm phoning Auntie Molly. I bet she'll come and help."

Angie went to the kitchen to put the last batch of scones in the oven. Emily collected plates and cutlery and started to set the tables and fold napkins. She went into the café terrace area and picked sweet peas and sprigs of rosemary to put in tiny vases.

Molly arrived and set to work whipping cream and putting an assortment of jam into tiny pots.

The café was quiet for once and the air was fragrant with the smell of fresh baking. In addition to scones, there were flapjacks and chocolate shortbread.

Angie and Molly were chatting companionably in the kitchen.

The café door swung open abruptly. Lacey stalked in. She looked like a cat on the prowl that had finally fixed its gaze on a mouse.

Emily stopped putting 'reserved' signs on the tables and stared at her.

"I want a word with you." Lacey's eyes flashed silver darts at Emily.

"What can I do for you?" Emily's heart was thudding but she tried to speak calmly and resist the urge to run for the shelter of the kitchen.

"You can keep out of my way and keep your hands off Richard Kingsley. He's mine."

"He's a grown man. He can make his own decisions." Emily glared back at her.

"Let me make this plain. If you don't stop interfering with my plans, then I'll have something to say to your public health department about this place. I could get you closed down just like that." She clicked her fingers.

"Does Richard know you're here? Or is it going to be like the time you phoned the Agency?"

Lacey glared at Emily, turned on her heel and flounced out of the café slamming the door so that the silver ornaments hanging on it rattled.

Emily sank down wearily on the nearest chair.

Angie emerged from the kitchen looking flushed and irritated. "

Angie emerged from the kitchen looking flushed and irritated. "You wouldn't think it would be possible to burn scones the way I watch them. Mind you – Nick did send me a text… Who was that? Why didn't they stay?"

It was Lacey, the American girl who lost me my last job."

"What did she want?"

"She was warning me off having anything to do with Richard."

"A touch of the green eyed monster eh?"

"She's threatened us with contacting the public health department if I have anything more to do with him."

"And doesn't Richard have any say in the matter?"

"It doesn't look like it."

There was no time to say anything else because a coach had just pulled up in the car park and a large group of ladies were getting off it and heading towards the café.

"Here we go then," said Angie. "This'll take your mind off things. You'll be too busy to think for a little while."

For the next hour and a half, Emily was kept occupied serving scones, pouring tea and coffee, whipping more cream and putting jam into dishes. The group were enthusiastic and asked lots of questions about Marchwood and the surrounding area.

"We've missed a trick here," said Angie. "If we'd had tea towels or tins of biscuits then we could've sold dozens of them. It's made me think we should have a small gift area near the till."

"You've not been the same since Nick sent you that article about marketing," teased Emily.

Angie laughed. "No – that's true. I'm seeing things in a totally different light. I definitely need a website for the café. Nick has offered to help me design one."

"That sounds as if it's guaranteed to take up a few evenings together," said Emily.

"Exactly," said Angie with a smug grin as she headed back to the kitchen.

Emily was pleased that Angie had found someone who suited her so well. She hoped one day she'd be lucky too but sometimes her feelings were too raw to allow her to feel she'd moved on yet. She wondered how long it would take her confused feelings to settle.

When she first arrived here she was feeling the pain of James's betrayal and not expecting to find true love again. She felt when she fled from London that she may never paint again. It took a new challenge from Angie to overcome that and allow her to move on. Also, moments of closeness with Richard allowed her to think that her heart wasn't frozen. However, she wasn't sure if it was her he really wanted or whether his feelings were anchored to the past and his dead wife.

She didn't know what the future held for her. All she knew was nobody was going to put her off her artwork again. She sat back down at the table and got out her sketch pad again, carrying on from where she left off at breakfast time this morning.

Thoughts spiralled through her mind. She'd need to earn a living from her artwork. She made a list. *Breakfast club for school children, after school art group, art group for adults.* She doodled trees and flowers around the edge of the paper, spirals of flowers like morning glories around hearts.

"That looks like a new departure for you," said a familiar voice.

"James," said Emily, feeling totally shocked. "What are you doing here?"

He looked the same as he always had – smart suit, expensive after-shave and a confident expression.

"I've missed you," he said. "I've not slept properly since you left London. You didn't stay around long enough for me to sort the misunderstanding."

They were the words Emily had longed to hear. Then a little voice in her head urged caution.

"What took you so long to get in touch?"

"I came looking for you. Your flatmates wouldn't tell me where you'd gone and I had my mobile stolen. Your number was on it." He had tears in his eyes and Emily felt sorry for him.

"You didn't trust me enough to look after you," he said.

Emily reached out a hand to touch his just as Angie emerged from the kitchen and came towards them.

"Angie, this is James," she said, giving her a meaningful look.

"Oh – James," said Angie. "Well I expect you two have got a lot to say to each other. I'll get you some coffees – you can sit in the flower bower if you like." She gave Emily a 'thumbs up' sign as she reached the counter.

Emily led the way to the trellis enclosed garden. As she entered the sweet pea and rose scented space, James took her in his arms.

"You look beautiful, Emily," he said. "I've missed you so much." His lips touched hers in a soft kiss.

These were the words that Emily would love to have heard a few weeks ago. Now she wasn't so sure.

Maybe it was the scent of the roses stirring up old memories and the pain of betrayal.

"I've got some money for you," said James, fishing in his wallet. "When you went away, I had no choice but to sell your stuff, particularly as I couldn't get hold of you."

"So how did you find me?"

"The article about this new venture of yours."

"It's not my venture – it's Angie's."

"But you're painting again – and you'll make a name for yourself just like you were before."

"So what are you doing with yourself?" asked Emily. "What brings you all this way from London?"

"Well, strangely, I was on the train to Worcester to chase up an investment opportunity for a client when I saw your article."

"Expanding your horizons are you?" Emily asked. She knew she sounded sarcastic but James didn't seem to notice. He'd always said London was the only place to be.

"Yes – things are going well. Beautiful spot this." He stretched back in his chair, putting his hands behind his head and looked up at the cloudless blue sky.

Emily looked at him, trying to imagine what she'd found attractive in the first place. Looking at him telling her about his latest business deals brought back all the pain of that last morning – his ex-wife, Claire, waiting outside the gallery and what she'd said about the previous history of the place Emily had thought of as her gallery.

She began to feel fidgety, wondering how many customers there were in the café and whether Angie was coping with them alright.

"I expect you'll want to make a move in a minute," she said.

"Yes – good idea," said James, his eyes lighting up with interest. "I'll just pop to the Gents first."

He'd left his mobile on the table. It bleeped with an incoming message. Emily didn't usually look at messages on other people's mobiles, but in this case she felt justified.

*"Don't bother coming back this time. I know you're cheating again. Claire."*

She looked around guiltily. She could see through the small window into the café that James was talking to Angie, even from this distance the charm oozed like treacle.

The phone beeped again.

*"James darling, where are you? I miss you. Becky."*

Emily got up and walked away from the table.

James hurried across to her, draping his arm around her shoulders like he used to. She remembered how it made her feel protected. Now it just made her feel irritated.

"I've squared it with Angie," he said. "She's happy for you to leave early."

"Leave?"

"Yes – let's go back to your place. We've got a lot of catching up to do." His voice was husky with desire.

"We can't do that," said Emily. "Nelson wouldn't like it."

"Nelson? Who is Nelson?"

"The new man in my life," said Emily swallowing back a giggle when she looked at his outraged face.

"That didn't take you long," he said. "I've come all this way to see you and see if we can make a fresh start and this is how you treat me."

"I thought you'd come here for 'business opportunities' – I suppose you could interpret that as preying on more women," said Emily. She looked at him and he squirmed under her scrutiny. "You had your chance James and you blew it – just like you have with Claire and goodness knows how many other women. Please don't bother me again."

"You don't really mean that," he said. "Let's go for something to eat, somewhere nice, and talk things over."

"There's nothing else to say. You're a liar and a cheat. I don't need you in my life anymore. The door's that way. Off you go."

There was a round of applause from Angie who had come closer to see how things were going.

The two women stood together, watching as James walked across the park towards the path that led to the town centre and the station. He didn't look back.

Half an hour earlier, Richard sat in the car park near the café looking at the trees that surrounded the play area and the pattern of leaves against sky. His intention was to call in at the café and talk to Emily just to see if her feelings matched his in any way. If they did, he had no idea what he could offer her. It was becoming clear that if the marriage to Lacey didn't go ahead, then he would have to sell the house.

On the way to see Emily he'd sat by Helen's grave thinking about the impact this would have on his life. The paintings and furniture in the house would have to be sold or given away. Worse than that, he would have to adjust to a different view from the window, not just on a temporary basis but forever. The good thing was Julia was too young to understand and would happily accept wherever he claimed as home. He was the one who would feel bad for the rest of his life for having to part with Oakwood House.

A shaft of light burst through the greyness above him. He looked up and it was as if there was a rainbow effect at the edge of the nearest cloud. Helen had always loved rainbows.

*"Don't stress about that, look at the rainbow, it won't last long,"* he remembered her say one day when he was getting worried about a work problem. He'd come and sat by her gazing at the rainbow until it faded away and when he'd looked back at what he'd been getting tetchy about he realised how unimportant it was.

For the first time since she'd died he had the feeling she was with him, encouraging him to stop being afraid of the future and move on. He watched until the rainbow faded, blew a kiss at Helen's headstone and headed back to his car.

He needed to talk to Emily and see if he'd imagined the chemistry between them the other day or if it was just the emotional circumstances that threw them together.

His gaze shifted to the flower borders and he focused on the bees browsing the geraniums and petunias in the flower beds near the ornamental fountain. He was opposite the bit of the café that Emily told him was called the 'flower bower' – a terrace enclosed by trellis smothered in honeysuckle, sweet peas and purple clematis.

There were gaps in the foliage so that customers could see the fountain and through one of these he was sure he could see Emily. Her dark curly hair was loose and she was wearing a red t-shirt. She was sitting at a table drinking coffee with a man in a charcoal grey suit.

Richard almost snarled with jealousy.

He wanted to march in there and take her away from there.

*"Grow up,"* he said to himself. *"That's probably a supplier she's talking to. In any case she's entitled to speak to whoever she likes."*

He got out of the car but resisted the urge to go any closer to the trellis. It wouldn't have mattered if he had, they seemed to know each other very well. The man was holding Emily's hands across the table and they clearly had lots to discuss.

Richard watched, feeling as if his heart was being ripped out, as they got to their feet and the man put his arms round Emily and kissed her.

The colours of the flowers blurred as Richard got back in his car and headed out of the car park.

Angie, heading out of the café kitchen to take the rubbish to the bin, recognised Richard's car and made a mental note to tell Emily later.

# CHAPTER SIXTEEN

The first things Richard heard when he arrived home and walked into the house were raised voices in the kitchen between Lacey and Ginny and the excited yelping of a dog.

He headed reluctantly towards the kitchen, all thoughts of going upstairs for a hot shower and a lie down abandoned.

Lacey and Ginny were facing each other, hands on hips.

"I take my orders from Mr Kingsley," said Ginny, "and he told me it was fine for Copper to come and stay while my sister is on holiday."

"Well, I'm not happy about animal food bowls in the kitchen. It's not hygienic."

"That's where they've always gone when he's stayed here before." Ginny had the now-familiar edge to her voice that indicated she'd been pushed far enough.

"He should be kept out in the yard."

"If you put Copper outside, then I'll be going as well."

Richard pushed open the kitchen door, trying to act as if he'd heard nothing of the tirade between the two women. They sprang apart and Ginny went back to peeling potatoes, her mouth set in a firm line.

At that point, Copper burst in through the open door of the scullery. This 'secret entrance' had become Julia's favourite since Richard had told her about how he and his sister Thea used to creep in and out that way. Even now, the door was rarely locked. The outside of it had a curtain of ivy – so it was becoming difficult to see it.

Copper yelped excitedly when he saw Richard and jumped up at him.

"Hello, Copper, how are you?" said Richard fondling his ears.

"Ritchie – your clothes!" said Lacey.

Julia raced in, her jeans and hands streaked with mud.

"Look at the state of you, Julia. Where is Maria? Why isn't she looking after you?"

"It's her afternoon off," said Ginny, "and Julia's been having a lovely time making mud pies with Copper. She'll miss him when he has to go home."

"Thank you so much for backing me up earlier," said Lacey after dinner when she and Richard were alone in the sitting room. She looked around the room. "Where have the new cushions gone? And why are those tatty ones back in here?"

"This is my house at the moment," said Richard, "and it's for me to decide what I have in it."

Lacey flinched, although he hadn't raised his voice.

"I have a magazine coming to take some photos tomorrow. It wouldn't look good to have photos of your ex around."

"Helen isn't 'my ex'. She was my much-loved wife. If she hadn't died in an accident we'd still be together."

"You don't know that for sure. My Dad's been married six times.

"I'm as certain as I can be."

"You can't go on putting her on a pedestal, making out she was perfect."

"She certainly was never that!" said Richard. "She was kind and loving, but she was also colossally untidy and scatty and used to drive me to distraction sometimes."

Lacey sank back in her chair, chewing at the knuckle on her right thumb.

"Why didn't you tell me about your father going for planning permission on my land? Why wasn't I consulted?"

"You've got plenty of land. Dad needs a flagship theme park in England. You'll hardly notice it."

"Are you kidding? Have you any idea of the damage you've done to my reputation by your steam-roller approach?"

"You'll have to accept my proposal if you want to stay here. My Dad says he'll buy the place anyway if you turn me down."

She got up, walked out of the room and slammed the door. He heard her footsteps on the stairs.

# CHAPTER SEVENTEEN

Richard overslept, mainly thanks to the extra glass of brandy he'd had after Lacey made her grand exit. He woke to the sound of more raised voices along the corridor. Realising he wasn't going to get any more sleep until the problem was sorted, he got out of bed, put on his dressing gown and headed in the direction of the noise.

This time the argument was between Lacey and Maria. It was the first time Richard had heard the Italian girl get mad – and she was so upset she was losing her ability to speak English.

"What's the problem?" he asked.

"*Ieri* – yesterday – Julia go into her bedroom," Maria pointed at Lacey," and she borrow ze silver lipstick."

"She stole it," snapped Lacey.

"Kids do stuff like that all the time," said Richard. "You can buy another one, surely."

"That's typical of you to condone bad behaviour." Lacey turned on Richard.

"Signor Kingsley – please listen," said Maria. "She," she pointed at Lacey again," was 'orrible to little Julia and made her cry. I thought I make things better for her. At bedtime we talk about things we do today. Then I wake up this morning and Julia is gone."

"What do you mean – gone?"

"She's hiding somewhere, attention-seeking as usual," said Lacey.

"Will you shut up and let Maria tell me about Julia." He took a deep breath and tried to calm the rising panic inside. There had been lots of people at the gates of Oakwood House – eager for news about the planning permission. What if one of those had taken her away. "When did you last see her, Maria?"

"Last night. I read her a story. I say goodnight to her and she go to sleep. Then this morning her clothes are gone, her teddy and her little pink rucksack." Maria dissolved into tears.

Julia felt nervous but determined to go ahead with her plan. She'd heard Lacey on the phone to someone yesterday and hadn't liked what she heard at all. Julia thought she sounded like the wicked queen in Snow White. She'd been told by Auntie Thea that eavesdroppers rarely heard anything good about themselves and it was true this time.

"Julia won't be any bother to me after the wedding," Lacey said. "She'll be going to boarding school. I'm sure it will make things easier for Richard – and he won't need to pay out for a nanny."

It wasn't the first time Julia had heard her say this, but over the last few days the atmosphere in the house had become as tense as an over-stretched elastic band that was about to snap.

Lacey seemed very certain she was going to marry Daddy and Julia didn't think it was a good idea at all.

She'd taken the lipstick from Lacey's bedroom to draw a special picture for her Mummy and write her a letter to ask if she could send Daddy a nicer wife. She'd left the letter in Daddy's study on her way out this morning.

Julia had woken up early. Her cousin Josh had taught her a trick of banging her head on the pillow five times if she wanted to wake up at five o'clock. They'd tested it out, creeping out of bed at Auntie Thea's and going downstairs to eat chocolate before the grown-ups were awake. Julia had tried it again this time and, judging by the pale light coming through the curtains, it had worked. She'd already packed a few things in her pink rucksack – her purse with her pocket money in it, her teddy, a book and some crayons, a drink and some shortbread biscuits she'd taken from the kitchen.

Maria had put her clothes ready and Julia dressed herself, trying not to make any noise. She hadn't had a wash but she didn't want the sound of running water to wake Maria. She brushed her hair, picked up her rucksack and went out of her room, careful not to bang the door.

Outside on the landing, she listened for any signs of life coming from the other rooms. There were none so she headed down the stairs and down to the kitchen, She went through the kitchen and into the scullery beyond that Ginny had told her was where the washing was done years ago. An old-fashioned mangle stood by the wall making it look like a kitchen in a museum that Julia had been to with Auntie Thea.

Copper, who was sleeping out there in his basket, yelped excitedly.

"Shush Copper, we mustn't wake anybody up."

It occurred to Julia that Copper would make a good travelling companion.

"Come on, boy," she said, clipping his lead onto his collar and pushing open the scullery door.

It was only when they'd almost reached the shelter of the woodland Julia realised she hadn't got any food for Copper. She didn't know if dogs liked shortbread biscuits.

They walked round the edge of the pond where the bulrushes grew and a white mist rose. The sun was just coming up – the pink and gold light creating rainbows in the mist that was like the smoke they used in pantomimes. Julia thought she could see people coming towards her in the swirling whiteness that smelled of Parma violets. For a few minutes she felt disorientated and lost.

Then the mist cleared and she could see the folly, the top reminding her of a bald head sticking out of a ring of green hair. It would make the most perfect home for her and Copper. She'd got some money in her purse so when the biscuits ran out she'd be able to go to town and buy some more. She didn't know what would happen after that – in the book Auntie Thea had read to them, the children found wild things to eat like mushrooms, berries and apples. They'd made camp fires and cooked the food themselves. Julia had made a bonfire with Uncle Adam and her cousins and they'd roasted potatoes in it. She was sure she could find enough wood to make a fire but she'd need to buy some matches when she went shopping.

Julia reached the folly and looked with dismay at the dense brambles around it. This was the closest she'd ever come to it and the brambles and ivy looked as dense as the thicket that grew up around Sleeping Beauty's castle.

At least nobody would find her once she got in there. It just looked as if that was going to take longer than she'd expected. She looped Copper's lead around a sapling and looked for something that might help her break down the nettles and thistles around the entrance. The door was open and the space beyond it looked dark and scary.

Julia found a big stick to bash the nettles and thistles with. She was glad she'd got jeans and a long-sleeved sweat-shirt on. Some of the thorns looked sharp. Copper barked excitedly when he saw the stick.

"This isn't to play with, Copper," she said. "This is to help me get in our house." She threw him a piece of biscuit and he chomped it enthusiastically.

It took a long time even with the stick and Julia's hands got scratched and sore. She stopped after a little while and ate one of the biscuits and drank some juice.

At last, she managed to create a little tunnel and squeezed through it into the darkness beyond. She'd get in first and then go back and untie Copper.

Greenish light filtered through the windows and Julia imagined this was what it would be like under the sea. It was cold and smelled like a church. She'd brought a blanket for teddy and wished she'd brought one for herself. Maybe that was something she could buy with her pocket money.

Julia edged forward on all fours. She was in the doorway now and could see a circular seat that ran all the way around the small building. The floor was made of blocks of stone that shifted unsteadily under her hands and knees. The cold rose up from what felt like gaps between them and made her shiver. There was a pattern on the floor that looked like a large star showing the compass points – north, south, east and west. They looked uneven and as Julia edged further forward, they rocked under her hands. It was like being on a strange kind of see-saw and she waited until the movement stopped. It stopped momentarily and then with a loud crack the floor gave way and Julia was catapulted down into darkness.

Two policemen arrived and Richard led them into his study. It was then that he found the letter Julia had written to her mother, the letters glittering silver against dark blue paper. "*Pleese send Daddy a nicer wife.*"

"This may be important," he said, his voice choked with emotion. "I was so sunk in my own problems I didn't think about her – didn't think she'd even notice."

"Had a lot of stress have you, sir?" asked the younger of the two policemen.

"You could say that."

"I was on duty the night your wife was injured in the accident," said the older policeman. "I was sorry to hear she'd died."

"Thank you."

Maria was called down, pale and trembling, and gave a full description of what Julia was wearing and what she may have taken with her.

Ginny knocked on the study door to say that the conservation protestors had heard about Julia going missing and had offered to help search the grounds.

"I think she's taken Copper with her," she said, "at least he's gone and so has his lead."

The two policemen left the study and went outside to brief the conservation volunteers. Richard watched as they set off in different directions. He went indoors to get his walking boots and Ginny coaxed him into the kitchen for a mug of coffee and a slice of toast. He looked at the pictures Julia had painted – mainly castles and princesses – all thick with glitter and wondered how he'd cope if he never saw her again. His eyes blurred with tears and he pushed the toast away from him. The thought of losing the house blurred into insignificance against the realisation that he may never see his beloved daughter again.

# CHAPTER EIGHTEEN

When Angie told Emily about seeing Richard's car leave the car park, she cringed at the thought that he may have seen her with James. She'd wished she'd known he was there and could've gone out and told him that a few seconds in James's arms had told her all she need to know. That her heart wasn't broken any more – and the only arms she wanted to be held by were Richard's.

"What would you have done?" Angie asked. "Lacey seemed pretty set on being number one in his life."

"I know. I just wish I knew what he wanted when he came here. Maybe it was to tell me about his wedding to her – but why would he do that? He's not made any promises to me."

"Maybe you should ask him."

"I couldn't," said Emily.

"Maybe he needs to know how you feel about him."

"It wouldn't make any difference if he's marrying Lacey, would it?"

Emily went home before her emotions got the better of her.

She arrived back at Laurel Terrace to find Ada sitting ghost-like in her armchair in the sitting room.

"Gran!" She hugged Ada, feeling relieved to see her grandmother. "When did you get back?"

"Early this morning. They woke me up to bring me home. Had a bit of trouble with Nelson – he didn't take to one of the ambulance men. The lady had to get

Molly to come and sort him out. She's given me a sandwich and told me to sit here till you got back."

"How do you feel?"

"Fit as a flea," said Ada. "Lot of fuss about nothing if you ask me. All those questions and the tests they did! I swear they thought I was a pincushion."

Emily went to the kitchen to make tea.

"Mind you," said Ada, "I've thrown them slippers away that I was wearing. I told you I should've got my new ones out but you wouldn't have it."

Emily swallowed down the comment she was about to make about Ada not wanting to wear the new ones because they were green and she considered the colour unlucky.

"I don't know what you've got against green, Emily. It's the colour of shamrocks and you know what they say about the luck of the Irish."

Emily, who was fairly sure the old slippers were to blame for her grandmother falling in the first place, wisely said nothing.

They had fish and chips for tea. Ada did full justice to hers whereas Emily only picked at her portion.

Later, when they were having their bedtime cocoa, Ada commented on Emily's anxious expression.

"You were looking happier – particularly with that nice young man in tow – and now you look all worried again. What's wrong, dear?"

"Nothing anyone can do anything about," said Emily, a lump coming into her throat.

She helped Ada up the stairs to bed.

"It's no good fussing over me like I'm made of cut glass," Ada grumbled. "A good night's sleep and I'll be running around like a two year old."

She looked at Emily over the neatly tucked bedcovers. "Your granddad always used to say to me: '*Ada, nothing you worry about will be any different for you losing a night's sleep. Decide what you're going to do first thing in the morning, make up your mind and do it and then close your eyes and forget it for now.*'"

There was a pause as Ada shifted on her pillows. "Mind you, there's things I should've said a long time ago and didn't."

"What sort of things?"

"It's too late to talk about those now, child. You need your sleep."

She looked like she did on the day Emily had asked her about the photo in her dressing table.

Emily went to her room, resolved to follow her granddad's advice. She thought about how good and steady he had been, his passion for old steam trains and how strange it was that was the only thing he and Ada didn't share. She'd never go by train if she could help it, claiming trains always upset her insides.

"You can't beat a good bus ride," was her view.

The next morning, after a breakfast of tea and toast, Emily carried a tray up to Ada telling her to stay in bed for a while. She had something she needed to do first thing and then she would be back to keep an eye on her.

"Go on with you, Emily," said Ada. "Molly's already said she's calling round this morning. Take as long as you like, I'll be fine."

She certainly looked more her old self this morning and Emily felt happier as she went back downstairs, fed Nelson and then, picking up her bag, headed out of the door. She'd already texted Angie to say she'd be in late – that she had something to do.

"*About time too,*" came the reply. "*Good luck.*"

Striding out purposefully, Emily headed towards Richard's office. She knew he was often in early – and she'd resolved to speak to him even if Lacey was there. When she arrived at the imposing house at the end of the High Street, it was to find that Richard had not yet arrived.

"Nobody's in upstairs as far as I can see," said the receptionist downstairs who'd given them the news of Lacey's arrival in England. "I feel sorry for the poor man – he's having a terrible time what with all the stuff in the paper and the wedding coming up."

"Is the wedding definitely going ahead?" Emily asked, her resolve failing.

"She thinks it is," said the receptionist, her face leaving no doubt as to what she thought of Lacey. "You can go upstairs and wait if you like. I can let you in."

"No – thank you," said Emily. She didn't fancy the possibility of Lacey arriving alone and finding her there. I'll call at his house."

"That's a tidy step," said the receptionist.

"I know," said Emily, "but it's a nice day."

"Not earlier on it wasn't. When I took my dog out earlier it was misty – more like autumn than summer…"

"Thank you for your help," Emily said again as she beat a hasty retreat. She had a feeling the woman would've kept her there all day chatting.

She headed towards Oakwood House, retracing the journey she and Angie made so many years ago when they were teenagers, excitedly clutching the bags that carried their picnic. She decided to keep to the main roads so that if Richard came along, she'd see him.

Emily tried to phone Oakwood House but the line was permanently engaged. She didn't have Richard's mobile number.

Her plan was to wait near the main gates in the hope of seeing him before he left for work. She reached the gates and found them closed and impenetrable. She pressed the buzzer next to them that linked to the house, but again there was no response. An avenue of trees stretched in front of her and she could remember driving along there with Richard on the day they brought Rufus here. She couldn't see the house from here, the foliage in the small woodland beyond the driveway was too thick.

Emily got her sketch book out of her bag. The marble dome of the little folly was visible from the main road. Maybe if she could sketch that she could create the rest of it from memory. The day she'd spent her with Angie was a jewel-like memory. They'd eaten their picnic in the folly, sheltering from the heat of the sun and then looked at a nearby pond that shimmered with dragonflies. Only the memory of Ada's anger had marred the perfection. Emily still didn't understand such an extreme reaction. Usually Ada would've laughed at escapades like that. Even Granddad's assurance that Ada had been upset about something else didn't ring true.

She sketched the dome and then got playful with the idea, re-creating it as a cartoon-style bald head struggling through the neck of a green sweater that was too tight.

The bushes around the folly had grown more but she could still see the strangle-hold of ivy and bramble and the rampage of a wild rose around the small building that must surely block the light – even if you could get in it, which Richard had said was not possible.

Tidied up, it would make a perfect love-nest Emily thought to herself, growing hot at the thought of being there alone with Richard, maybe when a storm was raging and they'd need to hold each other close to keep warm…

*"Stop it,"* she said to herself, *"he's not interested in you."*

Emily wondered how long she could loiter here by the gates. She'd tried calling Oakwood House again but the line was still engaged. There was no response to the buzzer.

She walked down the road a little way, trying without success to find the broken piece of wall where she and Angie had squeezed through. Since then that section of the wall had been renovated and the railings above it replaced to deter intruders. They did a good job, Emily thought. Even as a teenager she'd been afraid of heights and the thought of having to jump down from a great height would have put her off the adventure.

Emily turned sharply when she heard the sound of frantic yelping coming from the direction of the folly. A liver and white spaniel was barking and the sound of its distress tore at Emily's tender heart. She called to it but it appeared unable to move. As far as she knew, Richard didn't own a dog so she wondered if this one had strayed onto the estate somehow and got trapped by something. Emily had done some voluntary work with the wildlife trust and had seen animals caught in old-fashioned traps.

She watched for a few minutes but there was no sign of an owner.

Emily tried the number for Oakwood House for a third time as well as the buzzer on the gate. As there was no answer, she decided the only thing she could do was to get over the wall and help the dog. She scanned the nearest length of wall for a gap but the best she could find was a place where the railings at the top were kinked far enough apart for her to be able to squeeze between them. The wall was a little lower here and, positioning her bag across her body and fastening it so nothing fell out, she managed to scramble up.

The only problem was, having climbed up onto the wall, she discovered it was a long drop down on the other side. A feeling of vertigo flooded Emily making the scene in front of her whirl like a merry-go-round. She crouched on the rough stone wall, holding onto the cold black strands of metal, her hands slick with sweat.

The dog yelped again, the sound becoming more agitated as if it was in pain. The sound reminded Emily of the night when she'd found Nelson as a tiny kitten being tormented by a gang of youths. She'd been frightened on that occasion but sheer anger had propelled her forward and enabled her to rescue the terrified kitten.

*"You can't stay here all day,"* she told herself. *"You need to go one way or the other. Forward or back."*

Going back wasn't an option – she needed to get into the grounds of Oakwood House. She took some deep breaths to calm herself and then, moving slowly, turned herself so that she was facing the wall and could lower herself down as far as possible on her arms before she let go. Below her was rough grass which would be softer to land on than the tarmac on the other side of the wall.

Her arms felt wrenched out of their sockets with the effort, as she hung there. It was like getting into a cold swimming pool. There was only one way – one, two, three and in you go. Emily closed her eyes and let go.

Her right ankle jarred on impact, sending a wave of pain up her leg and her forehead hit a rock sticking out of the ground. She lay for several minutes feeling dazed and sick, unable to move, while the frantic barking of the dog continued. She dabbed at her forehead with a tissue. Fortunately there was no blood but it felt bruised. She pushed herself to her feet using the wall as leverage and stood waiting for her giddiness to subside.

The insistent barking of the spaniel encouraged her to move forward although every step caused pain through her ankle and her head. He greeted her enthusiastically and she noticed his lead had been looped around a small tree. She released him and he raced towards the folly and back then started rooting in Emily's bag.

"Sorry, I haven't got any food," she said. "Let's see who you belong to."

It seemed strange that he'd been tied up there but that there was no sign of an owner.

"Copper, is that your name?" The dog's tail thumped enthusiastically and he licked her hands.

There was a phone number and a postcode that suggested the spaniel came from Bristol. Emily rang the number but only got the mechanical tones of an answerphone. She left a message and decided the best thing she could do was take Copper to Oakwood House – if she could walk that far herself.

"Come on then," she said, but the spaniel showed no signs of wanting to go in the direction of the house. He was fixated on getting into the folly.

"Copper, come out of there," she said, making a grab for his lead and hobbling towards the patch of woodland.

Copper pulled her back towards the folly.

"What is it then boy? Show me."

Emily let go of the lead and the dog headed towards the place where she remembered the entrance of the folly was. It overgrown and wild but it looked as if someone had made an attempt to get into it. The nettles had been bashed down and some of the brambles had been pushed aside. The disturbance was recent because the leaves were still green. Emily couldn't imagine that a grown adult would've managed to get through the small gap that had been created that exposed the dark interior beyond. However, Copper wasn't going to move on until she investigated.

Emily edged towards the place where the brambles had been pushed aside. She could smell wild roses, damp vegetation and the musty old church sort of smell that emanated from the folly.

"Is anyone there?" she called, then laughed at herself for being so silly.

It felt like one of those 'haunted' games she and Angie used to play at Hallowe'en.

Then a cloud went over the sun and the temperature dropped, she heard a sound that was like the fluttering of a bird or a bat or the scurry of a mouse. She wondered if Copper had been chasing something and just wanted her to flush it out.

She felt nervous. It was easy to understand why Richard's grandmother felt this place was haunted. It was definitely spooky and the thought occurred to her that nobody knew where she was.

Emily was wearing jeans, a lilac t-shirt and a purple cardigan. The cardigan was thin and decorated with flowers the same colour as the t-shirt. It had been her latest charity shop 'find' and was now scuffed and torn from her escapades with the wall. Her jeans were now grass-stained and she reflected that she wouldn't exactly help her cause when she did catch up with Richard.

The strange sound came again – more like a whimper with an echo this time.

A flood of thoughts spiralled through Emily's mind.

"Who are you?"

The strange sound stopped. A sudden wind blew around the folly, skittering last year's dry leaves, rustling like silk against the cold stone.

Emily felt scared as she edged forward into the tunnel until she reached the small step that indicated the entrance to the folly. The door was pushed a little way open and it was difficult to move it any further. Emily wondered why. The small building was dark – she could only just make out the circular marble bench that ran all the way round. Then a sudden shaft of sunlight filtered through one of the stained glass windows near the top casting a spotlight onto what looked like a bundle of rags. A bundle of pink rags. A bundle of pink rags that stirred a little as if waking from sleep.

Emily thought of every horror film she'd seen and wondered what she was going to come face to face with.

The ground rocked unsteadily under Emily who was still on all fours. It woke the crumpled looking figure in the pink rags and Emily was afraid they'd both be catapulted downwards. She could see velvet darkness under the blocks of stone that made up the folly floor and could feel intense cold rising upwards towards her.

The figure whimpered again and raised its head, turned tear-stained eyes towards Emily.

"Julia – what are you doing here?"

"I've broken the floor in here and Daddy's going to be so cross."

Julia looked as if she was on an island of stones in the middle and Emily didn't know what was underneath – or how deep the drop was under the floor. The most important thing was to calm Julia down and encourage her to keep still.

"Daddy won't be cross. He'll just be glad to find you."

"He'll be very cross because he's marrying Lacey and she's going to send me away to school. And my arm hurts and I'm so very hungry and cold."

"Nobody is going to send you away," said Emily feeling alarmed at how pale Julia was. "Now I want you to do something very brave. I'm going outside to phone for an ambulance. Can you be a big brave girl and stay really still until I get back?"

Julia nodded.

Emily edged backwards out of the tunnel, her ankle feeling swollen like a balloon. She tried her mobile but there was no signal even when she moved a little way away from the folly. She didn't feel she could chance leaving her for the time it would take her to reach the house and get help. The stones looked too precarious.

She looked around for something she could use to help her. Copper was lying in a patch of sunshine, his head resting on his paws. The sun glinted on the links of his metal lead.

Emily called him to her and unclipped the lead, hoping it would be long enough. She crawled back into the enclosed space, relieved to see that nothing appeared to have changed where the state of the floor was concerned.

She leaned forward until she could touch Julia.

"We're going to play a special game," she said, her heart thudding. "First we need to put Copper's lead round your waist."

Julia giggled, making the floor move again. The giggle turned to a nervous whimper.

Emily moved herself back over the threshold of the folly to where she hoped it was safe, still holding the end of the lead. She hoped it would be strong enough to hold Julia even if the worst happened and the floor collapsed entirely.

"Now," said Emily. "For the next part of the game I want you to pretend you're a snowball rolling down a hill. As quick as you can roll across the floor towards me."

Julia hesitated.

"Tuck your poorly arm in so you don't hurt it any more. Shut your eyes. On the count of three. One…two…three."

It felt as if it was happening in slow motion. Julia rolled towards Emily raising a choking cloud of dust off the stone floor. There was a loud creak followed by a crash as some stones on the far side tilted and fell into the void below.

Julia was white and shaking in Emily's arms.

"Come along," said Emily at last. "Let's go and find Daddy."

Julia looked doubtful.

"It will be fine – I'll be with you." She took off her cardigan and wrapped it round the still-shivering Julia. Then she picked up the stick Julia had used earlier to bash the nettles and brambles to use as a walking stick as her ankle was now throbbing.

On the way back, Julia complained that her legs were tired and she felt poorly. There was a wooden bench in a sunlit corner at the edge of the wood, so Emily laid her on there, still wrapped in her purple cardigan. She left Copper with Julia.

"He can be the nurse," she said, making Julia smile.

Oakwood House looked as if it had as much drama going on as a disaster movie. Emily could see a police van, an ambulance car and a lot of banners protesting about a theme park. There was the sound of chanting and someone was shouting about intruders.

Lacey was at the top of the steps when Emily reached the house. She was wearing immaculate white – a total contrast to Emily's dishevelled state.

She strode towards Emily on impossibly high heels, spitting venom. "I knew you were behind trying to wreck things for me. This demonstration is all down to you isn't it? Look at the state of you. I'm going to get the police to throw you out."

"I need to see Richard. I've found Julia."

"I'm sick of hearing about Julia."

At that point Richard came out of the glass doors to the garden and caught sight of Emily.

"Richard." Emily stumbled forward into his arms. "I've found Julia. She was in the folly but I got her out. The floor's collapsed in there."

Richard turned pale. "It's my fault for not renovating the place."

"She's fine," repeated Emily. "She's on the bench down near the wood and Copper is looking after her."

The colour drained from his face as he called to the paramedics.

Then everything happened at once. Richard carried her through the glass doors into the sitting room where an agitated Lacey was in full drama mode.

"She can't come in here."

"She most certainly can." Richard placed her gently on the sofa where he'd put her on the day they brought Rufus here and issued instructions for Ginny to bring her a blanket. He raced off after the paramedics.

Emily lay on the sofa covered with the soft blanket Ginny had brought her.

"The paramedics want to check you over when they've seen Julia, otherwise I'd have brought you a mug of tea as well." Her smile was friendly. "I'm so relieved you've found Julia safe and well – and I'm sorry about your poor ankle. Have a good rest, you deserve it."

Emily focused on the photo she'd seen before in this room wondering why her grandmother would have had a copy of it.

At that moment a woman swept into the room. Her hair had the sleek, glossy look of a crow's wing and she was dressed as if she was going to a cocktail party. She wore chunky gold jewellery and smelled of exotic perfume. She carried a clipboard and a mobile phone and was issuing instructions to someone following her who looked strangely familiar to Emily.

"Nick!" Emily sat up, still huddled in her blanket.

"Emily." His face broke into a smile. Then his expression changed. "Emily, what's happened? You look like a road accident."

Lacey glared at Emily. "I'm sorry about the disruption, but can we get on with things?"

"With respect," said Nick, "there doesn't seem to be anything to get on with since the wedding isn't happening." He turned to Emily. "Does Angie know you're here?"

"No. This morning has been an unexpected adventure." Emily felt shaky, the shock finally setting in as to what could have happened and how things could have ended very differently. She took a deep breath. "Anyway, what's happened with you? I thought you were taking a job in Scotland. Angie was really down about it because she thought you weren't coming back."

Nick flashed her a boyish grin. "There have been a few changes between us– as of yesterday. Then Camilla (he indicated the sleek dark-haired woman) was let down by her photographer and called me with this job."

Camilla gave Emily a broad red lipsticked smile. "Are you the Emily I keep hearing about? The artist who works with Angie in the spectacular pink café?"

Emily nodded.

She noticed with a wicked grin that Lacey had left the room in a huff – her departure apparently unnoticed by Camilla and Nick who were enjoying the coffee and cake Ginny had brought them and discussing their next job.

Richard returned carrying Julia in his arms. He settled her down on the sofa under the blanket with

Emily and she curled up next to her like a puppy and promptly fell asleep.

He knelt on the floor by Emily and took her face in his hands and kissed her tenderly on the lips. "The paramedics will be here soon to take you both to hospital." He shivered and took her hands in his. "I could have lost you both."

"You didn't," said Emily kissing him back. "We're still here."

There was the sound of a series of bumps out in the hall. Nick went to look.

"It seems as if Miss America is bringing a lot of luggage downstairs."

"I could have told you from the start that romance wasn't going anywhere," said Camilla in her cut-glass accent. "But you and Richard, my dear Emily, you rock." She gave Emily her business card. "Let me know how things go – I'd like to know, whether *Brides Today* covers the story or not."

In the midst of the drama with ambulances and police vans, Lacey was trying to book a taxi to take her and her mountain of white and gold luggage to the airport.

She looked forlorn and sad, her bubble of arrogance finally burst.

"I'm sorry things didn't work out between us," said Richard kissing her on the cheek.

"I knew deep down as soon as I got here it could never work. I guess I've always been used to getting my own way."

"I've spoken to your father and he's switching the planning permission to one of the old factory sites in town. It will give him far more scope for his ideas."

"Thank you," she said quietly. "Emily's a lucky girl wherever you end up living."

The taxi arrived and then Richard was distracted by Ginny letting him know that Julia and Emily were about to be moved to hospital.

Lacey's departure made Richard feel as if a huge weight had been lifted from him.

"I'm sorry things didn't work out with Lacey," said Emily as they waited while Julia had her arm plastered. Emily's ankle was fortunately only sprained and there were no signs of concussion.

"It would've been a way of keeping Oakwood House," said Richard.

"So why didn't you marry her?"

"This girl with liquid amber eyes and a passion for cute furry animals came into my life unexpectedly and stole my heart."

Richard's mobile bleeped with an incoming message. He'd already had several from Andrew Crane which he'd not yet responded to.

"So what happens about the house?" asked Emily.

"Does that mean you won't want me if I'm not living in a big house?"

"No, silly. I'd live with you in a caravan."

"Do you mean that?"

"Yes," she said, "of course I do."

"I just can't believe I won't be living there anymore."

"Have you really thought of every possibility of keeping it?"

"Andrew Crane and I have had countless meetings about it."

"Could you turn it into apartments?"

"We thought of that but the cost would be too great."

"If you're forced to change your view of the world then make the best job of it you can."

"Who said that?"

"My grandmother when I returned from London feeling lonely and sad when my relationship with James broke up."

"If he was the guy you were with the other day in the flower bower at the café it looked as if things were going pretty well."

"Appearances can be deceptive. I'm glad he came to see me because I found out what a two-timing rat he was. I just wish you'd called in to see me and not just driven off."

"I thought you didn't want me – and I can't believe how sad I felt. I was going to come and find you this morning and then Julia had other ideas as to how the day was going."

Julia came out of the plaster room with the nurse who'd taken her in there. She was still clutching Emily's cardigan like a security blanket and there was a purple cast on her arm.

"You and your wife can take her home now," the nurse said to Richard.

Emily and Richard exchanged secret smiles.

"Hey, how come you've got a purple cast when your favourite colour is pink," said Richard.

"Purple is my new favourite colour, Daddy. I'm grown up now."

They walked along the corridor where Emily and Richard had shared a close embrace after Ada had been admitted to hospital. The smell of food drifted up the stairs from the canteen.

"I'm very hungry, Daddy," said Julia.

"I think we all are," said Richard as they headed down the stairs for pasties with chips and beans.

"You can't beat proper Cornish pasties," said Richard. "Helen and I always said if we hadn't lived at Oakwood House then we might have moved to Cornwall."

"There'd be nothing to stop you doing that now," said Emily, realising as she said it how much she'd miss him.

"Would you come with me?"

A smile lighting up her face was all the answer he needed.

Emily's mobile rang and he watched as a cloud crossed the sun and her face changed from happy to anxious as she listened to the person calling her.

"Tell her I'll be home as soon as I can," she said.

She pushed away her half-eaten plate of food and struggled to her feet, limping as she stood on her injured foot.

"What is it, what's the matter?" asked Richard.

"It's my Gran – Ada. Her neighbour Molly has just been in to see her and she keeps asking where I am. She says she's got something urgent to tell me before she dies." Emily's eyes filled with tears. "I asked Molly if she needs to be in hospital and she said she's not feeling ill, just guilty about something. What can my Gran have to feel guilty about?"

"We'll soon find out, won't we?" Richard got to his feet, scooped Julia into his arms and held out his hand to Emily. "Come on, the car's not far away."

The journey passed in a blur of hedgerows and traffic flashing past. Emily focused on her grandmother being alive, well and her usual self when she got there. Julia chattered for a bit and then fell asleep, her thumb in her mouth, despite having stopped the habit for some time.

Before they set off, Richard had phoned Ginny to let Maria know where they were and what was happening next.

"It's been like Paddington Station here since you left," said Ginny. "People in and out all day long and reporters camped outside the gates waiting for you to come back."

"What are they doing that for? I've made a statement that the theme park is now going ahead in the old factory quarter. Why don't they push off there instead? "

"You've not heard then?"

"Heard what?"

"I'll wait for Andrew Crane to tell you. It's a change to hear him with good news for once."

Ginny wouldn't say anymore – other than Richard needed to hear the news for himself.

He started the engine and headed towards Marchwood, hoping Ada didn't have bad news for Emily. She looked as if she'd been through enough for one day.

# CHAPTER NINETEEN

Ada was sitting in her chair looking neat and tidy in a black skirt and blue jumper with a glittery brooch.

Her neighbour Molly was fussing in the kitchen when Emily, Richard and Julia arrived. Richard decided it was best to go there first rather than head back to Oakwood House and drop Julia off. There was no telling what he might get involved with if he did so.

"It's the man with two names," said Molly coming in with a tray of tea and biscuits. "And I haven't met this pretty young lady."

Julia blushed prettily and hid her face against Emily's sleeve.

Emily took her grandmother's hands in hers. "What's the matter, Gran? Molly said you'd had a funny turn."

"Funny turn be blowed! It was no such thing. I just had a funny feeling about you all day and it got me thinking about something I should've told you about years ago and didn't because it never seemed to be the right time – and I was worried you'd think badly of me."

"Why would I ever think badly of you, Gran after all you've done for me?" Emily looked into her grandmother's eyes. "What did you do that was so bad? Steal a packet of dolly mixtures from the sweet shop?"

"A bit worse than that," said Ada. "I've held onto something that didn't rightfully belong to me for a lot of years. It was when you said something about your young man here losing his home I thought to myself it isn't what Jack would've wanted to happen. The more I thought about it, the worse I felt – that's why I got Molly to call you."

"You called me Jack before," said Richard – when I called to see Emily and found you lying in a heap at the bottom of the stairs.

"Well, you look so much like him it gave me quite a turn, made me think of how things might have been if they'd worked out as we'd planned." Ada took a bite of lemon cake. "Not that I'm looking back with any sort of regret, please don't think that. My Frank was a good man and we had some wonderful years together. It's just that sometimes I wonder what might've happened…"

"You're talking in riddles, Gran. What do you mean?"

"Go upstairs for me Emily and bring down the wooden box that's on my bed."

"Can I go too?" asked Julia who was fascinated by Ada's glass-fronted cabinet full of ornaments.

Ada had promised Julia could come back one day soon and have a proper look at them.

"This is like a real-life doll's house," Julia said to Emily as they went up the steep cottage stairs. "Is this where you sleep?" She insisted on seeing Emily's bedroom and then Ada's.

"Come on," said Emily. "Let's take the box down."

"What's in it?"

"I have no idea."

Emily handed the box to Ada. She stroked it lovingly.

"When I first brought it back here I hid it under the floorboards under my bed and that's where it's stayed. Then I got to thinking about what happened if I died and I hadn't told anyone about it – and then the house was sold or pulled down like they keep threatening."

At that moment the rattle of the cat flap announced that Nelson had returned. Ada looked worried. "He doesn't like men and he definitely doesn't like children."

Emily prepared to defend Richard and Julia from attack, but to her surprise, the cat purred loudly and made a beeline for Julia, settling down next to her in the blue armchair. Julia stroked his ears.

"Why has he only got one eye?" she asked.

"He had an accident when he was a kitten. Emily rescued him."

Nelson purred for a few more minutes and then fell asleep.

Richard's attention had been drawn by the photos on Ada's mantelpiece. There were photos of Emily when she was a child, and Ada's wedding photo, black and white with an elaborate spray of flowers and white lace veil. But it was the last photo that caught his attention.

"May I ask why you've got a photo of my Great Uncle on your mantelpiece?"

Emily noticed it for the first time.

"That was the photo that was in your jewellery box, the one you wouldn't talk about."

"I finally got a frame for it," said Ada. "I should've done that a long time ago."

"So what's in the box?" asked Emily.

"It's a relief to tell you," said Ada, taking a gulp of tea. "I did tell Frank of course – he knew the whole story from the beginning." She looked at Richard. "Pour us a brandy, would you dear," she said to Richard. "I think we could all do with one – apart from Julia of course."

He did so and Ada began her story.

"Jack and I met after the war. I worked in the local cinema and he bumped into me, literally, when I was on my way to work. He was very apologetic and offered to take me out for afternoon tea by way of apology. We didn't go out together in Marchwood, of course. That wouldn't have been right with him living at Oakwood House.

If my mother had found out, she'd have been hopping mad."

"Where did you go?" asked Emily.

"Before we discovered somewhere closer to home, we used to meet a couple of stations down the line at a little café in Brampton. Nobody knew us there. It was so romantic."

Ada took a sip of brandy.

"Jack had survived the war – he didn't expect to – he'd ended up as a prisoner of war. When he returned to Marchwood he realised how limited his options as a third son were. I know you're probably thinking badly of me, but this wasn't a hole-in-the corner affair. We really loved each other."

Julia had fallen asleep with Nelson still cuddled up against her.

"I've never seen him do anything like that before," said Ada, "not even with Emily."

"Tell us what happened next, Gran," said Emily. "How old were you?"

"I was twenty. Jack was thirty five. He asked me if I felt we could have a future together. I said yes, but not here. England was a lot more class-conscious then. The Kingsley family would never have accepted me."

Richard protested about this.

"I'm sure you're not like that dear, but it was a different world back then." She stroked the box on her lap as if it was a living thing. "At Christmas, he proposed to me in our special meeting place and he gave me this box. This is all I have left of him but I've never been able to wear it – only on my own under the moonlight." Ada's eyes looked luminous with tears.

"Don't tell us any more if it's upsetting you, Gran," said Emily.

Ada flapped her hand at her. "I need to tell you. I hope you won't judge me too harshly," she said looking at Richard.

He reached across and took her hand in his.

"We arranged to meet at seven in the morning on Valentine's Day at Marchwood Station. *'Bring the necklace I gave you,'* he said. *'I'll arrange everything else.'* He didn't turn up and I thought to start with that he'd found somebody else and that this" – she lifted the lid – 'was a fake."

Richard and Emily gazed in wonder at the silver and ruby necklace in the black-velvet lined box.

"You used to meet in the folly," said Emily, the truth dawning. "That's why you were so cross that day when Angie and I had been trespassing there. And you waited at the station and Jack didn't turn up so that's why you'd never travel by train."

"It upset your grandfather," said Ada. "He loved his trains. He was there on the day I was waiting. Two hours I stood there until my feet felt frozen to the platform."

Tears were running down Ada's face. "It was two days before I found out what happened. Frank came to tell me. He looked so serious my mother told me to invite him in. She thought that was who I'd set my sights on. "Ada," she said, "if I'd known it was a good, honest man like Frank Brookes you'd set your heart on I wouldn't have spent these last few weeks worrying." It seems she had a feeling I was into something I shouldn't be – thought the films I was watching were turning my head. "Well, Frank and I did marry the following year. Nothing was going to bring Jack back. But it hasn't stopped me wondering how things might have turned out. He said he'd got everything planned. I've often wondered where we were going."

"The only reason he didn't turn up to meet you was because he died of a heart attack in his bedroom," said Richard. "There were two passenger tickets for the *Queen Mary* going to Canada in his pocket as well as confirmation of a booking at The Strand Palace Hotel. We always wondered who the other person was."

"I only ever had the necklace and one photo to remember him by," said Ada. "His trunk was returned from the station eventually," said Richard. I don't think anyone ever bothered to unpack it – it's probably still in what used to be his room."

"I'd love to see it," said Ada. "The nearest I got to the house was the folly."

"The folly's a nasty place" said Julia waking up. "That's where I fell down."

"The floor gave way," said Emily. "It was quite an adventure for both of us today."

"Always seemed solid enough when we were there – mind you it was a long time ago. Seventy years."

She looked at the necklace again and touched the stones lovingly before closing the box and handing it to Richard. "Jack always said this would be useful for a rainy day. I gather yours has already arrived and I'm sure you'll make better use of it than I will."

Richard swallowed back tears. If the necklace was worth as much as it was reported to be then his money worries were well and truly over. He got out his mobile and sent a text to Andrew Crane and also to his sister Thea. *'Rajah's necklace back in the Kingsley family.'* He fully expected a return phone call from both of them asking if he'd been drinking.

It felt appropriate to carry on having a party, but there obviously wasn't room to do so at Ada's house.

Richard rang Ginny and said he was bringing a few visitors. When he explained what had happened, her joyful whoop could be heard by everyone in Ada's sitting room.

They headed back to Oakwood House and stayed up late into the night drinking wine and eating toasted cheese. The necklace was much admired by Ginny before being locked in the safe for the night. Ada got to see the portraits in the hall of Joshua Kingsley and his wife Elizabeth, the original owner of the Rajah's necklace.

Best of all, Ada got to sleep in the bed that had once been Jack's and to see the tickets that would have taken her to Canada so long ago.

The following morning there was more good news. The previous day, one of the paramedics who had taken a look in the folly had noticed something unusual about the gap under the floor. With Richard's permission, he contacted a friend of his who was an archaeologist.

The archaeologist lost no time in asking Richard to take a look at what he'd found. Some distance below the floor of the Georgian folly was what looked like a

Roman mosaic. "There's evidence to suggest there were several villas in this area," said the man, his face flushed with excitement. "It could put Oakwood House well and truly on the map."

When Richard returned to the house it was to the news that Andrew Crane was waiting in his study.

"Emily's with him. She's taken him coffee," said Ginny. "She is lovely," she added with a smile.

"I know," said Richard softly.

"He was chuntering on about needing to get the house on the market. Emily did try to tell him this might not be necessary now, without giving away your news."

"He obviously didn't get my text yesterday," said Richard, pausing to collect the necklace from the safe hidden behind one of the smaller pictures in the black and white tiled entrance hall.

He made his way along the corridor to his study.

"Ah, Kingsley, there you are." For once, Andrew Crane wasn't pacing about. It looked as if he and Emily had been enjoying some light conversation. "Now you're here it's time we got on with sorting out the next stage of the proceedings."

"That may not be necessary," said Richard, laughing inwardly at the startled way that Andrew Crane pushed his glasses further up his nose and stared from him to Emily and back again. "We're awaiting confirmation that a Roman mosaic – and possibly part of a villa – are underneath the folly. Also, the missing necklace has turned up. Look!"

The ghost of a smile lightened Andrew Crane's sharp features. "In that case, Mr Kingsley and Miss Randall, I think a small celebration might be in order."

# EPILOGUE

## February 14th 2017

The archaeologists investigating the mosaic that was visible under the folly had exciting news. The site was bigger than expected and they said that in time the remains of a whole villa would be uncovered.

The folly was going to be moved, piece by piece to a new site.

"I'm glad you're not pulling it down," said Ada. "That place was very special to me and Jack."

"It was special to my grandmother as well," said Richard. "She spoke of seeing Roman soldiers here. Maybe the people from the past were trying to tell her something."

The plans for the development of Oakwood House included a nature trail. A charge was going to be made for entry with lots of interesting things featured including a wigwam for storytelling, a picnic area and a pets' corner, featuring frequent visits from Rufus – the You Tube rabbit.

After the plans for the theme park were abandoned, Richard got in touch with Lacey's father and suggested he bought one of the old factory sites in Marchwood. Work on this was going ahead and it looked as if the area where Ada grew up would at last get the face-lift it needed.

Richard had designed a new studio and gallery for Emily, together with a tea room which Angie had agreed to manage.

Ada had moved in with Emily and Richard, occupying the room that once belonged to Jack.

Camilla at Brides Today magazine was captivated by the 'double romance' and decided it would make a most unusual feature.

The real celebration happened the following February when Emily walked down the aisle of All Saints church to become the second Mrs Kingsley. It was an early spring day of sunshine and showers. The churchyard was full of snowdrops and yellow aconites.

Unlike Lacey who had had her celebrity style wedding three months before in New York, Emily wore a simple white lace dress she found in a charity shop and a garland of flowers. The dress had been a subject of discussion between her and Richard.

"We can afford for you to spend a little more on a dress," he'd said when she'd shown him her special purchase.

"I don't want to," she said. "Our story began with a charity shop dress and this new chapter will begin with one. It feels – lucky."

She was wearing the copy Richard had made of the rajah's necklace. The original had been sold to offset the outstanding debts.

"It's a pity we couldn't have kept it," said Richard.

"We've kept the house," said Emily giving him a soft kiss, "and I can wear this one as often as I like." Julia, dressed in purple chiffon, and enjoying her special place as a bridesmaid was already talking enthusiastically about wanting a baby sister instead of a rabbit.

"It's what people do when they get married, Daddy," she said.

"Is it now," said Richard sharing a secret smile with Emily as they looked across at each other.

The wedding service was beautiful, the church packed with guests. Flashes of sunlight poured in through the stained glass windows, the light catching the red stones of Emily's necklace and the red and cream roses she carried.

As the service ended a spattering of raindrops hid the windows of the little church. Emily smiled as she heard Ada whisper that a bit of rain on a wedding day was a sign of good luck.

As she and Richard emerged from the church to greet their guests and face the barrage of cameras a perfect rainbow arched above Oakwood House – the sign of a happy future.

The End

Thank you for reading
'The Girl With Amber Eyes.'

For details of my other publications,
writing courses, talks and critique service
please see www.writers-toolkit.co.uk

Follow me on Twitter @SueJohnson9

22198244R00111

Printed in Great Britain
by Amazon